All Sales Final

All Sales Final

C.M.W. Hawkins

Undead Avian Publishing

AN UNDEAD AVIAN PUBLISHING
PUBLICATION

First Edition

10 9 8 7 6 5 4 3 2 1

Set in Georgia & Thunderstorm

ISBN 13: 978-0-9952100-7-3

Printed through IngramSpark

Follow Undead Avian Publishing on
Social Media:
https://www.facebook.com/undeadavian/
https://twitter.com/undeadavian

For my Patrons

1

"Attention River Park Mall shoppers: The River Park Mall will be closing in fifteen minutes. We will reopen tomorrow at nine am. Thank you for shopping with us today, and have a pleasant evening."

I checked the time after the announcement blared overhead. Either my watch was five minutes slow, or the mall's clock was five minutes fast. Either way, I rolled my eyes and hurried towards a kiosk selling miniature remote-controlled cars.

My nephew was having a birthday tomorrow, and I still hadn't bothered to get him a gift. Mostly because I had very little idea about what a seven year old boy would like besides mud and bugs. I was seven once, but it was nearly thirty years ago, and all I could remember was mud and bugs. If I showed up to the party with *those* my sister would have a conniption.

"Hi there! How can I help you today? Looking to buy a remote-controlled car?"

Christ, I wasn't even within ten feet of the kiosk and the saleswoman was already heading my way. She must've seen the desperation in my eyes and knew I'd be an easy mark. I hated to burst her bubble, but this sale was going to be quick, easy, and cheap.

"Uh, yeah. Look, I just want whatever you've got around ten or twenty bucks, hopefully in blue or green."

Her exuberant smile faded a little, the brightness in her eyes dimmed, and part of me felt a little guilty. I got it, really I did. Sales meant paychecks. For all I knew she was the owner of the damn kiosk and this was her livelihood. Still, I had my own tight budget to worry about, and I wasn't about to spend more than twenty bucks on a kid I saw no more than twice a year.

"Yes, of course. That would be these ones right here. However, if you notice, they have a wire connecting the car to the remote, which really limits what they can do. These ones right here are the same color," she pointed at a set just above the cheap ones, "but they come with wireless remote *and* rechargeable batteries."

"How much?" I asked hesitantly.

"This line is fifty dollars."

Fifty bucks for a car that was no bigger than my thumb. A car that probably cost no more than five bucks to make and three bucks to ship. I tried to haggle.

"I'll give you thirty-five."

The way her brow scrunched up, you would've thought I told her to drop her pants and think of Christmas; a mixture of confused and offended.

"Sir...we don't negotiate. The price is fifty dollars, *plus tax.*"

She made a point of emphasizing the tax bit, and and I took in a breath and let out a sigh.

"Just give me one of the twenty dollar ones."

Her smile was completely gone now and she grabbed one of the yellow ones. I opened my mouth to correct her on the color when the automated overhead announcement rang out again.

"Attention River Park Mall shoppers: the River Park Mall is now closed. Please finalize any purchases and make your way towards one of the exits. We will reopen at nine am tomorrow. Thank you for visiting with us today, and have a pleasant evening."

The saleswoman had been talking during the announcement, but I missed what she'd said. I assumed she was giving me the total.

"Here," I said, as I handed her a twenty dollar bill.

While she took the money, I watched a group of teenagers milling around a trash can at one of the exits. I couldn't see what they were doing from this distance, but I got lost in thought watching them. And then the saleswoman cleared her throat.

"Sir? There's tax. The total is twenty-one sixty-eight."

I pulled a one hundred dollar bill out of my wallet and her demeanor became even more annoyed.

"I can't break this. Do you have anything smaller?"

"No, I don't. What do you mean you can't break this?" Now it was my turn to be annoyed.

I had a feeling she was trying very hard not to roll her eyes at me. The back of my neck started to itch and my ears got hot. She just stood there, staring me down. I had a feeling I was getting played for a sap, but the mall was closed and there was no way I'd have time to find an ATM or another open store in time.

"Alright, you win. Give me the car for fifty."

Immediately her bright, happy smile returned and she reached for a green one "Oh, I'm so glad you changed your mind, sir!" She spoke excitedly now. "I am sure your son will be very happy with this."

I was so annoyed and aggravated that I didn't even bother to tell her it was my nephew. I just gave her the money and was slightly irked that she didn't ask for tax *this* time. She handed me the bag, that same damn smile beaming on her face.

"Don't forget to tell your friends!"

"Uh-huh."

Bag in hand, I hurried towards the exit, brushing past the group of teenagers. I saw now why they were huddled around the trashcan: they'd set the thing on fire. I snorted a laugh to myself and continued out the exit. Oh, to be young and stupid.

The night air felt refreshing against my face. The mall had felt stuffy and overly warm, and the change in temperature was just what I needed to help me cool off after the encounter at the kiosk. I closed my eyes, took in a deep breath of that fresh air, and let it out again.

Still basking in the quiet moment of relaxation, a commotion from behind caused me to open my eyes and turn around. It was the same group of teenagers barreling out of the exit, with two security guards right on their heels. The kids weren't looking where they were going and ran right into me, knocking me on my ass. I heard a crunch as one of them stomped on the bag holding the car. One of the guards stopped to help me up as the other one gave chase, yelling and cursing at them.

"You little shits better run! If I catch you I'm calling the cops!"

"Sir, are you alright?" The guard helping me up seemed genuinely concerned.

I looked down at the bag, picked it up, and my heart sank as I heard it rattle. So much for my nephew's present.

"Oh, geez. That is really unfortunate." He looked down at the bag. "How about I get you inside to fill out a report. If you've still got the receipt I can give you a mall credit for what it was worth. You can buy a new one tomorrow."

I glanced at my watch again. It was just barely after nine, but if the woman was still around, there was a chance I wouldn't have to make an emergency stop tomorrow.

"Lead the way."

He smiled and nodded, probably glad I wasn't threatening to sue, and began to head back inside. I followed after him, but not before glancing back and looking up at the moon. It was full that night, but the color seemed off. It had a slightly purple hue, something I'd never seen before. A shiver ran down my spine and I shook it off. I wrote off the feeling as just nerves and annoyance and caught up to the guard.

"My name is Frank. I'm really sorry about what happened to your..."

"Toy car," I finished for him. "For my nephew."

"Yeah, real shame. The security office is just over this way, past the restrooms."

The rest of the walk was made in silence. I had always been the type to keep to myself, speaking when spoken to and keeping things simple. I hated idle small-talk with someone I didn't know. I always felt that the only people who would be honestly concerned with the small details of my day *weren't* going to be total strangers. Before the silence became awkward, we reached the office and he let me inside.

"Excuse the mess, we don't normally get visitors," he chuckled, amused at his own little joke. I got the feeling he said that every time someone who didn't work here was let in.

The 'office' itself was little more than a wall of monitors with a desk, a few lockers in one corner, and a table with a few chairs in the middle. He motioned for me to take a seat and dug around through some papers inside one of the desk drawers, pulling one out and pushing it towards me with a pen.

"Alright, just fill that out Mister...?"

"Hamilton. David Hamilton."

He smiled. "Alright David, just fill that out, give me the receipt, and we'll get you squared away."

Nodding, I did as I was told. It was a standard incident report form, and I described what had happened as best I could. I decided to omit the part where I got played for a sap while buying it. After I finished, I fished into the bag for the receipt, but couldn't feel it.

I dumped the bag out, little bits of broken car bouncing and rolling every which way, but no receipt fell. I turned the bag inside out and cursed to myself.

"You *do* have your receipt, right, David?"

"The woman at that kiosk...I don't think she gave me one. That happens, right?"

"And just what 'kiosk' did you acquire that from, sir?"

Sir. As soon as he began to call me sir, I knew I had been switched from victim in need to annoyance at closing time. Rolling my eyes, I did little to hide my aggravation at the situation.

"That one by the exit those kids trampled me at. There was a woman who sold these stupid cars for fifty bucks."

"You really expect me to believe this," he motioned towards the pitiful pile of plastic parts, "is worth *fifty* dollars?"

"You better! I didn't ask those kids to break it! I just wanted the twenty dollar one, but she wouldn't break a hundred, so I had to buy this piece of shit!"

My anger was rising, and so was my voice. The guard had the gall to place his hand on the pepper spray at his side like he was about to get into a shoot-out.

"You need to calm down, sir. Look, I can tell you're agitated, and if this woman can corroborate your story, we can get this all sorted. Let's go for a walk."

He ushered me out of the security office, and walked two steps behind me. I could feel his eyes on me the whole time as we made our way back to the kiosk. My worst fears were realized as I saw that the whole thing was closed up and locked, and the woman was nowhere to be found.

"This is it, but she's not here."

"I can see that, sir. I am very sorry this happened, but you will need to take it up with the owner of the kiosk and see if they'll be able to help you. Since there is no proof of purchase, I am currently unable to assist you. Come back tomorrow first thing. I have an early shift and we can try to figure this out then. Please make your way to the exit."

"*Unable to*...look here, you goddamn rent-a-cop, my purchase was broken, you promised to accommodate me, and now you're basically telling me to fuck off!"
"Sir, lower your voice and lose the curse words."

"No! I will not lower my goddamn voice! I've been cheated and all I wanted was that stupid, fucking, twenty dollar car!"

"Sir, you need to vacate the premises before I ban you from the mall."

I was getting hot headed, and I knew if I kept pressing this I was going to end up on the losing side of things. Hell, I already was, judging from the small crowd of employees and last-to-leave shoppers who were starting to gather. I took in a deep breath and decided to just cut my losses. I'd try again tomorrow before the party.

"Fine," I spat out through clenched teeth. "I'll be back tomorrow."

I turned on my heel and headed towards the same exit as before, when I saw the saleswoman burst through the doors and back inside. Something seemed off about her appearance, but I was just happy to see she was still around so I wouldn't have to return to this damn place in the morning.

"There she-"

The remaining words died in my throat as I realized *why* her appearance felt off. Her white shirt was now red and her hair was slick, looking like she had just gotten out of the shower. But it wasn't water: she was covered in blood. Her eyes were wide and frightened, and as soon as she saw me she started to scream.

Good god, did she scream.

Her voice died down and the lights flickered as she collapsed into a heap. What was only two or three seconds felt like an eternity of silence, then everything happened at once. A few people, including the security guard I was with, ran to her side. Some of the bystanders began to scream and panic on their own, and a couple more ran deeper into the mall.

As for myself, I was stunned. Not twenty minutes ago this woman had been annoying me with her damn sales pitch and now she was there, on the floor, covered in blood and blubbering like a baby.

"Move back! I'm a doctor!"

A man, who looked to be in his early fifties, ran by me and pushed aside the people who were huddled around the woman. He started to examine her, yelling at the others not to move her. This snapped me out of my own stupor, and I forgot about trying to get a new toy car. I let the bag fall to the floor and moved to look out the door she had come in.

Being summer, days were far longer than normal, and even though it was after nine, it should still be rather bright out. 'Should be' was the phrase that stuck in my mind, as it was currently black as pitch outside.

This was uncanny. Even in the middle of a moonless night, the lights in the parking lot should light up the whole area. Just looking out into the dark expanse was making my eyes hurt and my brain itch. It wasn't right, and it certainly didn't seem natural.

I glanced at my watch to double check the time, but the hands weren't moving. I tapped it a few times and, when they remained stationary, I cursed under my breath. I had just bought this two weeks ago.

"I...I can't find any wounds..."

The doctor's mystified words drew me back to the group and I was thankful for the distraction. Something about that darkness gave me an uneasy feeling, and I wanted to stay where it was well lit for the time being.

There were six people immediately surrounding her, including the security guard and the doctor. Glancing over to the right, I saw a group of seven or nine people, watching from a safe distance and waiting for the prognosis. Smart people. So why was I compelled to get closer?

The doctor was on his knees, his hands covered in blood, and he kept looking her over, examining her neck, face, abdomen and legs for injuries. I assumed he was double checking his findings, as he was moving more methodically now, and less like someone trying to save a life.

Shaking his head and taking in a breath, he let it out slowly. "She doesn't have so much as a scratch on her. This isn't her blood."

"We need to get out there and find whoever could be injured!" Frank spoke up, jumping to his feet and pointing towards the doors.

"I wouldn't go out there. Something is...different," I warned him.

"Where is Daniel?" Frank asked no one in particular, ignoring me. "Did he come back into the mall after chasing those kids off?"

Those gathered either shook their heads or shrugged. Most of them didn't know who he was referring to, and the doctor was far too concerned with the woman on the floor to give an answer. I wracked my brain, trying to remember if the guard had gotten back inside before it got dark. Frank and I came inside, went right to the security room, and then back out to the kiosk. I never saw the other man at any point after we came back into the mall.

"I think he's still out there."

As the words escaped my mouth, Frank's face took on an alarmed look. "This could be his blood! I've got to see if he's okay!"

Before I could tell him about the strange darkness outside, he ran towards the entrance and threw open the doors. I took a step after him, then another, finding myself following him. Maybe he'd have a reason for why the lights in the parking lot weren't on. Maybe something to do with that flicker from before. There had to be a perfectly reasonable explanation for all of this.

My hopes for rationality and reason were dashed as I caught up to Frank, just a few feet past the entrance. This particular entryway was slightly recessed from the rest of the mall exterior, and had a large walkway that led to the sidewalk. He was just standing there in the middle of it, mouth open slightly as he stared into the void.

"There a reason the lights are all off in the parking lot?" I asked him, begging for some sort of logical explanation. I knew immediately from the look on his face there would be none.

"Where...where the hell did they all go?"

His voice was barely more than a whisper as he walked slowly towards the main sidewalk. I couldn't explain it, but the closer he got, the more uncomfortable it made me. I was about to tell him we should head back, when a gurgling noise came from around the corner to the left.

"Daniel? Daniel!" he called out as he set off to explore. Everything in me screamed that this wasn't where I should be right now, so close to whatever the hell that darkness was, but part of me also didn't want to leave him alone out here. To leave *myself* alone out here. I ran to catch up, and was a few feet away when he turned the corner.

"Jesus Christ!!"

He yelled and stumbled, trying to slow himself, but I was hurrying to catch up and there was no way I could stop in time. I collided with him. We both fell into a heap on the sidewalk, and I saw what had startled him so much.

At first I couldn't understand what I was looking at. I looked as if it were just a pile of meat someone had left out. But, there were pieces of fabric stuck to it that appeared to be the same sort of clothing Frank was wearing, so it was easy to assume this was what was left of Daniel. The pool of blood he was crumpled in seemed to still be growing, and the stench was overpowering. I couldn't tell from his position if we were looking at his front or his back. I turned and retched, using the side of the building to steady myself.

"D-Dan?? What the fuck did those kids do to you?!"

I barely noticed Frank pull out his pepper spray and wield it as a weapon. Whatever had done this to Dan wasn't about to be stopped by some spray.

"Don't you...have a gun?" I choked out, wiping bile from my lips with the cuff of my jacket.

"No! They don't let us carry in the mall. Too much of a safety risk."

As Frank's gaze kept darting around like a panicked animal's, I thought I noticed movement coming from Daniel. But...there was no way that pile of meat was still alive. As if to defy my thoughts, it sat up and turned to looked at us. There could be no doubt anymore that this had been Daniel; I could see his name badge. I could also see that his entire face was gone, down to the bone. Empty eye sockets stared at us as he reached out and opened his hands. In each fist was an eye.

Frank and I were both too stunned to move as Daniel rose. A portion of intestine fell from his gut and hit the cement with a wet slap. It took everything in me to choke down the vomit rising in my throat again. He turned his head to Frank and opened his mouth.

Instead of words, silence. Daniel clenched his jaw, then began to open and close it, over and over, as he looked at Frank. Daniel took one step forwards, causing Frank to cry out in terror and use the pepper spray.

The liquid squirted over the skull, completely missing the target. The figure stopped, as if perplexed by Frank's reaction. It cocked its head to the side, teeth still chattering, and then lunged.

I could barely register what was going on. I kept pushing my back against the wall, vainly hoping the building would just swallow me up and save me from this waking nightmare I found myself in. Frank tried to get away, to run from Daniel, but the bloody figure was far too quick. It grabbed onto his shoulders, lifted him as though he weighed nothing at all, and tossed him into the dark.

For a moment I thought I was safe. That the figure would follow Frank into the black expanse and give me a chance to run back into the mall, back to safety. But Daniel's head turned and looked directly at me. I knew I was fucked.

A scream started to form in my throat as abject terror gripped me like a vice. As it escaped my lips Daniel moved a bloody finger to his teeth, right to where his lips should have been, making the 'shhh' motion.

I could only stare, transfixed, at the ghastly visage of what used to be Daniel, until something large hit the wall next to me. I glanced over and saw that it was Frank. He had slammed into the wall, and was breathing hard, looking even more terrified than I felt. He was covered in blood, clutching one arm against his chest; his hand and most of his forearm were missing. He barreled past me and Daniel, and ran back to the mall.

I didn't want to share his fate and made a break for it as well, but Daniel reached out at the same moment. He managed to grab onto me, but his hand was covered in blood and my jacket easily slid free of its grip. Glancing back to see if he was following, I watched as he slid into the darkness without a sound.

Once we were both inside and I had slammed the doors shut, Frank leaned against a wall, breath coming more and more raggedly as he slid down.

"What are you...Dear God! What happened to his arm?!" the doctor yelled.

"L-Lock the...the door," Frank got out through clenched teeth.

I looked at the doors, made of nothing but pieces of metal and sheets of glass and wondered if locking them would actually accomplish anything, but I did as he asked. Daring to look to where Daniel had disappeared, I saw nothing, which was somehow more frightening.

After securing the doors, I turned around. The doctor was on Frank, treating his injury and checking his vitals as everyone else stared at us. The woman who had been covered in blood was sitting up now, leaning against her kiosk and wearing someone's coat. Her face was blank as she stared at the floor.

I moved away from the doors as the others silently con-tinued to stare, and took a seat next to Frank as the doctor worked to stabilize him and his arm. I took in a shaky breath, let it out slowly, and found the words pouring from me far eas-ier than I thought they would have.

"Daniel is dead, and I'm pretty sure that's his blood all over her." I motioned towards the woman, who still hadn't looked up. She was either deep in shock or her mind had bro-ken from the ordeal. It was a wonder my own mind hadn't shattered.

"What happened?"

I looked towards the voice and saw that the speaker was a worried-looking young woman. She was shorter, with numerous facial piercings and shoulder length hair, dyed sev-eral different colors. She bit her lip and waited for some sort of explanation, but I stopped as I realized even I didn't fully com-prehend what had just happened.

"I...We were attacked by something out there. Frank got tossed into the darkness, and came back without an arm. Beyond that, you'll have to ask him."

"We can't," the doctor spoke up, adding to the conver-sation.

"Why not?"

"Because he's dead."

III

"We need to call the police!"

"I can't get any bars on my phone!"

"What the hell is going on?!"

"I was in the middle of a call and it cut out."

Voices were erupting around me as true panic started to settle over the group of people. No longer were they in shock about what had just happened, just desperate to find help or to escape.

As they carried on, I looked over at the doctor, who'd moved Frank's body so that it was laying flat on the ground. There was another man with the doctor; I assumed it was his son, due to the similarities in their facial features. He had taken off his jacket and laid it over Frank's upper body. A pool of blood was forming quickly underneath.

I'd only known Frank for a few minutes, and in that time he had come across as nothing more than a rent-a-cop on a power trip. Regardless, I never would've wished this fate on him, or anyone else.

"We need to get out of here!"

The speaker was an older man, with thinning blond hair and a mustache that sat crookedly on his face. He was so thin it looked like a strong breeze could knock him over, but his voice was surprisingly commanding. I looked up at him, shaking my head, as others repeated his sentiment and made their way towards the door.

"You can't. It's far too dangerous, and you saw what happened to Frank," I said, pointing towards the body.

"Don't think you can stop us! We need to get to the parking lot, and get the hell out of here before whatever maniac did this comes back!"

The crowd was getting more and more worked up with this idiot's rantings. I felt like I should do something to stop them, but I had no idea what.

"I don't know what happened out there, but I know this man is dead. His forearm was broken in half and then *ripped* off. Whatever 'maniac' is out there is capable of rending limbs from body, and I personally feel safer with it out there, and myself inside."

The doctor rose as he spoke, taking a handkerchief from his pocket to wipe some of the excess blood from his hands. The man with the blond mustache stopped to look at him, and for a moment I thought he would listen to reason. Instead he sneered.

"Who's to say they aren't already in the mall?! There are tons of entrances, and none of them are locked!"

He had a point, as loathe as I was to admit it. The mall wasn't huge, but each side had several entrances, including those of the large department stores. There was no way we could secure them all, even if we wanted to.

"We need to find someplace safe then, immediately." The doctor spoke up.

"Fuck you. I'm not staying here a moment longer." The man moved past the doctor, who grabbed him by the arm. "Get your hands off me!"

"I can't stop you, but I'm telling you right now: I'm relocking those doors after you leave." He paused, as if to emphasize what he said next. "*I won't let you back in.*"

The man jerked his arm free and, without saying a word, went and unlocked the door. A few of the people that were following him hesitated, but that didn't stop him as he marched outside.

Their group consisted of eight people, including the blonde man and the woman with multi-coloured hair. At first, only five of them marched out confidently. They made it about halfway to the edge of the darkness before the remaining three decided it was safe to follow. After they were all outside, the doctor went and did just as he promised, locking the door and heading off towards the left.

"Alright. Those of you who are still here, we need to search for others, try and convince them to stay, and lock this place up tight until help can arrive."

"Do you really think it's safe?" A teenager in a yellow and black jacket spoke up, his voice cracking. Whether from puberty or stress, it was impossible to tell.

"For now, who knows? We need to find a phone, and see if we can call out. If not, then we need to find a place we can remain until help comes," the doctor responded.

The sound of the entrance door rattling violently caused everyone to jump. The only two unfazed by it were the saleswoman, who was still sitting and staring at the floor, and the doctor.

I looked back and saw the woman with the colorful hair, a smear of blood on her cheek and tears running down her face.

"LET ME IN, PLEASE!!"

The doctor just folded his arms and stared at her.

"What about do no harm, huh?"

While he had said *he* wasn't going to unlock the doors, I had never made the same promise. I ran over and turned the lock, letting her inside. I was expecting several more people to follow, but there was no one else. When I looked past her, I could see why.

Daniel had come back out of the void, and was in the middle of tearing someone apart. When he ripped off the head, I saw that it was the man with the blonde mustache I looked, but couldn't see any of the remaining members of their group. They must have scattered once Daniel began to attack. Only the woman had the sense to head back to the relative safety of the mall.

I watched as the thing that had been Daniel dropped the corpse and turned towards me, its eyeless sockets seeming to stare at me. It raised its fingers to its teeth again as it faded back into the darkness. A thought blossomed in my mind, logical and terrifying. I suddenly had an idea as to what his purpose was in all this.

"He...He's keeping us in here."

The doctor was standing next to me. I didn't know how long he'd been there, but he had to have seen the same thing I did. His face was set, and it was impossible to tell what was going through his mind.

"That is...As long as he's out there, we need to stay inside to remain safe," he stated, and then headed over to his son. They began to speak with one another in a hushed tone I wasn't able to overhear.

I looked around at who was left inside. The woman with the rainbow hair, the kid in the yellow jacket, the doctor and his son, the saleswoman, a young couple, and a woman in a wheelchair. When the doctor didn't take charge again, or start giving out a plan, all eyes turned to me.

I really didn't want the mantle of leadership. It gave me awful anxiety, and made me clam up. But the adrenaline pumping through my system, coupled with the thing Daniel had become, superseded any social anxiety I might've felt as I began to speak.

"We should introduce ourselves."

I glanced at the woman on the floor, but figured she might not be the best person to begin with, so my eyes fell onto the woman with the multi-colored hair. Her gaze met mine, and I could tell we were both thinking the same thing: this is some seriously fucked up shit, and we're stuck right in the middle of it.

"Uh...my name is Emeline."

A second of silence followed, then another. When it didn't seem like she was going to offer anything else, the teenager spoke up. He was almost as tall as I was, thin build, with jet black hair. He was Asian, but I couldn't tell what nationality.

"I'm Shawn-"

The doctor interrupted him as he and his son joined the rest of us. "Look, I agree that we should introduce ourselves to one another, but perhaps now isn't the best time? We're still in front of these *clear glass* doors and need to see if we can lock down the mall and find anyone else who may be trapped here."

Shawn looked a little dejected that he didn't get to finish, but I agreed with the doctor. I suddenly felt vulnerable standing there in the open and moved away from the doors, but not before looking back outside. Other than the gore and blood stains, there was no indication that Daniel had come back.

"What are we going to do about her?"

The man from the young couple pointed over at the saleswoman, and I couldn't help but feel sorry for her. She was still wearing blood-stained clothes, and hadn't looked up from the floor since she sat down. I moved over towards her, got down to her level, and spoke softly.

"Hey, we're going to go see if we can find anyone else. It's probably better if you come with us."

No response, aside from the sound of her breathing, and the occasional sniffle.

"We'll head to Hannigan's Department store first. See if we can find you some clean clothes."

I held out my hand, right in front of her face, and I saw her jaw clench. I was about to give up and just head off when she grabbed my hand. Hard. I helped her up, and repositioned the coat so it was over her shoulders again. She never looked up from the floor, but she also never let go of my hand so I took it as a positive step and headed towards the others.

"We need to hit Hannigan's to find her some clothes," I told the rest.

They looked at her and nodded, but the doctor was the first to speak. "Just as well. We should move from one side of the mall to the other, making sure we lock doors as we go."

Turning on his heel, he moved towards the corner of the mall where the department store was located and the rest of us followed. Fortunately, the store wasn't far from this entrance, though I remembered that it had several entrances itself, being on the corner of the mall.

"Why don't we just find a store with a rolling door and lock ourselves in? It's got to be a lot safer than relying on glass doors for protection."

The young man spoke up, directing his question at the doctor, who kept walking. His son was the one to respond.

"If we can lock down the whole mall, we'll have access to food, water, and shelter. If we just pick a random store we'll be cornered."

The young man seemed to accept this as a plausible reason and no further questions followed. I, however, was less convinced. Why was it important to have food and shelter for

an extended period of time? While what was happening outside defied any logical explanation, help had to be coming once
people realized we were missing. This was a busy mall, and at
the very worst we'd spend the night before being discovered by
workers coming in for the early shift.

I decided to keep my mouth shut. The doctor and his
son had taken charge, and were only trying to keep people protected, and feeling safe. I did my best to ignore the unease coa-
lescing in my gut. As long as we stayed safe, everything would
turn out okay in the end. Plus, there was nothing to stop us
from hunkering down in a store somewhere once we got supplies.

"HELP! HELP!!"

The yell broke me out of my own thoughts. It was coming from ahead of us, but the echo made it impossible to tell
exactly how far. It did, however, confirm that there were still
other people still in the mall.

"Over here!" The woman in the wheelchair motioned
towards an electronics store a few stores away from our position, with an older man standing just inside, waving his blood-
stained arms frantically.

"Are you injured?!" The doctor began to examine him
immediately.

"No, it's my friend. He's hurt real bad!"

I looked inside the shop, trying to locate his friend, but
I didn't see anything other than a smear of red across the
linoleum floor. It led behind the register counter. I took a step
forward, but the saleswoman gripped my hand, tight enough
for me to hear a small pop. I looked back at her and she shook
her head at me, biting her lip.

"It's alright, I'm just going to see if he needs help."

As I tried to reassure her, I saw her eyes widen with
fright. I thought maybe she was beginning to have another
episode and turned to the doctor, only to see that his eyes were
just as wide. In fact, everyone looking into the store had the
same look on their face. Slowly I turned around, dreading what
was behind me.

There, behind the register, was a thing like Daniel. It's
skin had been torn off like his, but this one's abdomen was already empty of guts and organs. Also, the arms had been nearly stripped of the meat, leaving just tendons connecting bones.

It stared at us with eyeless sockets, then raised a finger to its teeth. Someone behind me screamed.

IV

The doctor's son looked frantically around for some sort of weapon as I helped move everyone out of the store and back into the mall itself. When I turned around again, he had found a metal pole, part of a display case, and was rushing at the thing.

He swung at it, missing once, before connecting with its skull. The sound, and how easily the skull ruptured, reminded me of videos I'd seen online of people attacking melons with hammers and baseball bats. A sickening thunk followed by a splash of thick material flying against a wall.

Instead of falling from the blow, the thing remained standing. The doctor's son took another swing. A bloody, skinless hand, moving with inhuman speed, grabbed the pole before it connected, and tore it from the the son's grip. He began to scramble backwards, trying to escape the creature.

"Reggie!!" The doctor yelled for his son, rushing towards him.

There was literally nothing any of us could have done, even if we had been standing right next to him. Instead of swinging the pole, as I think Reggie anticipated, the skinless creature thrust it forward, impaling him through the face. The end of the pole jutted out seven or eight inches from the back of his head, protruding just above his left ear.

"NO!"

The doctor yelled for his son, rushing to his side as the younger man fell to the ground. My jaw dropped when he started to scream in pain. *Jesus Christ...he's still alive.*

I ran forward and grabbed the doctor by the shoulders. I didn't want to give that thing a chance to kill him, too. "We have to get out of here!"

"Not without my son! I can save him!"

Looking up, I saw the skinless man advance from behind the counter, moving with ease. Whatever force was animating his body was also acting as his eyes; the thing deftly walked over items scattered across the floor as it made its way towards us.

"Then bring him and let's go!"

"If I move him, he could die!"

Reggie had stopped screaming, and, glancing down, I could tell he was either dead or in shock to the point he was unresponsive. Even the best doctor in the world wouldn't be able to save him now. I couldn't imagine the pain the doctor was going through, but it would be the last thing he ever felt if we didn't get out of there.

He was sobbing, saying Reggie's name over and over again, and I decided that the only way to save his life was to literally drag him out. Grabbing onto his shoulder, I pulled roughly. He immediately began to struggle.

"Unhand me! I need to save my son! I need to save my son!!"

It took some effort, but I managed to get us back to a safe distance by the time the thing stopped next to his son. Everything fell quiet, and I thought it would grab the pole, or finish the job, but instead it just stood there, motionless. Even the doctor had stopped and we all watched with morbid curiosity to see what it would do next.

The creature did nothing. Reggie's body, however, defied reason. First, he sat up, as if nothing was wrong. Then he began to pull the pole from his head.

"No! Don't pull it out, son, you'll bleed to death!"

Reggie continued, ignoring his father's plea. Once the pole was out, blood gushed from the wound, soaking his shirt. He then pushed his fingers into his eye sockets, popping his eyeballs out with unnerving ease. Watching it happen made me queasy, and I had a strong feeling I knew what was going to happen next.

"We *need* to get out of here!"

I had to agree with Shawn. I had no interest in watching Reggie skin himself, but I also had no wish to be followed by those things. Most of the stores were still open, but a few were already locked down for the night. I looked around the electronics store and saw that it, too, had the same sort of security. I prayed it was the kind of door that locked automatically once closed, and jumped up to try and bring it down.

"Anyone know how to work these doors?!"

The sound of wet tearing behind me, and the looks of horror on everyone's faces, was not the answer I wanted. *Shit.* There had to be a latch, or a release, or a button *somewhere.*

There! On the wall was a set of green and red buttons locked in a plastic box. I rammed my elbow against it, and was immediately thankful that whoever installed it had opted for cheap plastic as it crumbled from the blow. I slammed my thumb into the green button and the door began a slow descent.

I looked to see if the doctor had come to his senses, but he was still on the floor, blubbering about his son. I grabbed for him, and tried to drag him towards the exit; he shrugged me off. Whatever was left of Reggie was pulling its own skin off in strips, and I had to will myself to stay focused and not vomit right there.

"He's dead! We need to go before we get locked in!"

The door was already halfway down, and I didn't want to risk stopping it. If he didn't get up in the next few seconds and follow me, he'd be trapped inside with those things and there would be nothing we could do for him.

I waited a beat and then tried again, but he ripped his arm away, actually moving closer to the creatures.

"Fuck it. I tried," I muttered under my breath and ran out, diving under the rapidly closing door. Another five seconds and it was shut. I heard a click as the lock engaged itself. It was a solid steel door, instead of the chain variety, so there was no way to tell what was happening on the other side.

I turned away, feeling sick to my stomach not only for what I had witnessed, but for having to leave that man behind. He'd just watched his son die, and then had seen some force mutilate the body. I should have tried harder.

Something large slammed against the door, causing it to rock in place, but it did not buckle. Blood started to flow from underneath it. Far too much blood, far too quickly. The doctor had to be dead.

"What the hell is going on here?!"

It was the old man. He looked as confused as the rest of us, but suddenly all eyes were on me. The doctor had been the self-appointed leader, and now he was gone. Why was I being singled out as his successor?

"I have no idea. But if more of those things are inside the mall, we're all in grave danger."

"We need to stick to the plan. We'll continue to head over to Hannigan's and search for more survivors."

The woman in the wheelchair moved forward, pivoting her chair back in our original direction. She gave her wheels a push and started off, without waiting for the rest of us. We had no other plans yet, so staying the course seemed the best option. I followed after her and the rest fell into line, silently.

The department store was a good five or ten minutes from where we were, but no one said anything. What could we say? We'd all just seen a man killed before us, then watched that *same* man sit up again and begin to skin himself. Normal conversation didn't seem appropriate after witnessing a sight like that.

"I'm Charles. Charles Fremont."

The old man had broken the silence, and I looked over at him. Aside from the blood on his hands and clothes, he reminded me a lot of my grandfather. He had a well-trimmed, white beard to match his white hair, a bit of a beer gut, and he was wearing a red polo shirt and black slacks. That's when I realized that he was actually wearing the uniform for the electronics store. He was an employee.

"Back there, who was that?" I asked.

"My manager. We've also been friends for about seven years. God...what happened to him?"

"No idea. But the same thing happened to one of the security guards." I replied.

"If we're going back to introducing ourselves, I'm Alex Dunham and this is my wife, Sarah. We've been married for about eight months."

What was it about newlyweds that caused them to want to tell everyone their name and how long they'd been married all in the same breath? I did my best to hide my annoyance. I gave a polite nod and smile. Sure, people were dying and turning into hellish killing machines, but please, do tell me how long you two have been sharing a bathroom.

He didn't look older than twenty and had short brown hair. He was wearing a t-shirt, jeans, and a thin green jacket. She had long blonde hair and was wearing a sundress. I looked at her shoes, heels.

"Maybe lose the shoes." I motioned towards her, pointing. "If we need to run, you could twist an ankle."

A look of worry spread across her face as she reached down to unfasten them, pulling them off and taking her place at her husband's side again.

That left the woman in the wheelchair. She had short black hair, was wearing a black shirt, and her jeans were tied off just below the knees. When a minute or two passed and she didn't offer her name, I decided to ask. "What's your name?"

When she didn't answer, I walked up next to her and asked again. "Name?"

"Heard you the first time. What does it matter?"

"What if we need to yell for you or something?" Shawn insisted. "We can't just call you cripple."

A few of us glared at him and he got a sheepish look on his face as he shut his mouth. The woman, however, barked with laughter.

"Shit, kid. You know how to lighten the mood. I'm Irene. Now that we've all shared with the rest of the class, can we please focus? Hannigan's is just around the corner."

Shawn laughed at her comment, but I didn't feel amused. By any of what was happening. I didn't have time to dwell, however. As we turned right, following the mall path, there it was: the entrance to Hannigan's Department Store. Only the ground level was accessible from the mall, but there was also a second level, and most likely a basement or maintenance area.

Everyone looked haggard and rough; I doubted any of us would ever go back to having a normal life once this was over, especially the saleswoman. She remained close to me, and I had begun to feel protective of her. I hoped she would recover from whatever shock she was experiencing, but for the moment I didn't mind; the role of protector gave me a distraction.

As we approached the entrance an odd thought crept into my head: with all the screaming and running we had been doing on our way here, why hadn't we seen or heard anyone other than Charles? Plus, the inside of Hannigan's looked as vacant as the rest of the mall had been. Had everyone gotten out, or had something happened to them, like Charles' manager?

I tried not to focus on such negative thoughts, and took point as we headed inside. The anti-theft alarm system began beeping as we all walked through and I felt my heart stop. The blaring noise was enough to wake the dead, and we'd likely be among them if we didn't shut it off, immediately.

Thankfully, the beeping stopped as soon as we'd all passed through; if I had to hazard a guess, someone among us had a penchant for the five-finger discount.

"It's probably just a glitch. If we're *lucky*, it won't go off again." I eyed Shawn as I spoke, my personal biases getting the better of me, but the truth was there was no way to know for sure who had set it off. I just hoped my message got through: I could give two shits if one of us was a thief; I just didn't want it to end up killing me.

The department store's mall entrance was next to the men's clothing and the escalators were to the right, next to a giant sign stating that Housewares and Electronics were upstairs. I honestly had no idea where to go next.

Irene brushed past me, heading towards one of the exterior entrances. I started to call after her to stop, or be careful, but she was moving too fast. By the time I got the first word out she had already turned a corner and disappeared down the walkway.

"I hope she's locking the place down," Alex muttered. "We should head in the opposite direction and do the same."

"What good is locking *glass* doors going to do?" Charles didn't sound enthused.

"Would you rather we make it easy for anything to get inside? At least this way we can hear when a glass door shatters," Alex explained. Thankfully, it was a better reason than 'because it makes me feel better,' which is what I would have said.

Charles nodded slowly, seeming to accept this. We moved as a group down the path opposite the one Irene had taken, when she came rolling quickly back towards us.

"Did you loc-"

"Keep your voice down!" She interrupted me with a harsh whisper.

I shut up immediately, and waited for an explanation. She stared back over her shoulder for a good twenty seconds before turning to face us. She spoke in a low, hurried tone, her breath coming in gasps from her exertion.

"There's another one of those things in here, and more outside. I nearly lost my shit, but the one inside turned to me and shushed me. I didn't make a sound, and then it *turned away.*"

"It what?!" Shawn's words echoed in the empty store.

"I said keep it down!" Irene growled back. She continued, "I dunno why, but maybe if you're quiet, they leave you alone."

"Could you see outside? Is there any way to get out of here?" Alex sounded desperate, and I noticed he was holding his wife's hand hard enough to make her fingers go white.

"Just more of that black shit. I watched a few of the dead guys go in and out of it, but it's impossible to tell what's on the other side."

At least we had confirmation that whatever was outside surrounded the whole mall. Thoughts of escape dwindled as I tried to think of what we should do next. I wasn't made for this leadership stuff. Maybe I could push Irene into it.

"What do you think we should do next?"

She shrugged, looking as lost as I felt. "Dunno. We still have power somehow, so maybe find someplace safe we can lock ourselves in. Keep them out."

We all looked at one another. Just twenty minutes ago we had been ready to go and find survivors, even fight back. Now we were all scared shitless and part of me just wanted to find a hole to curl up in. But at the same time another fear started to well up deep inside. If we hid, there was a chance we could be cornered. I didn't want to die here, waiting for help that would never come. Or worse, at the hands of those things.

"We need to keep trying to get out of here, or find help." I stated. "How much food or drinkable water do you think is *in* this place? We might last a week or two, but then we'll die of dehydration or starvation, assuming those things don't get us first."

Charles spoke up. "We can find a safe spot first, then some of us can forage for supplies. Once we get settled, we can figure out a plan."

The group nodded and murmured their agreement to the idea, and we all started to leave the department store. This time the alarm was silent; perhaps my words from earlier had been taken to heart and the person responsible for the first alarm had dumped their ill-gotten gains when the rest of us weren't paying attention.

Once back in the mall, we quickly found one of the mall maps and considered our options. None of us wanted to be anywhere near the electronics store, and the department stores were too large to defend properly. If we picked a place near the food court, though, it would make getting supplies easier.

There was a large arcade right next to the restaurants. The map was hardly to scale, and it was impossible to tell how big it really was, or how defensible it would be, but I was eager to make a decision. The longer we walked around the mall the more exposed I felt.

"We would be safe here," Irene stated, pointing at a sporting goods store.

It was much closer to where we were now than the food court was, and my guess was it would also have a rolling door, like the electronics store, instead of several glass ones. Not to mention weapons. While the pole had done little to stop the thing from killing Reggie, just having something in my hands would make me feel better.

"Let's put it to a vote."

"AAAAAAAAAAIIIIIIIIIIIEEEEEEEE!!!!!"

The saleswoman's piercing scream surprised everyone, and I almost shit myself. Looking around frantically, I saw four of the 'Shushers' standing at the entrance to Hannigan's. All four placed their fingers to their non-existent lips, then ran towards us.

"Hurry! Get to Sports N'Stuff!" Irene yelled as she took off like a rocket.

I grabbed onto the saleswoman's hand, jerking her out of her stupor, and followed after Irene. No need for a vote now.

It was difficult to run while holding onto the woman's hand; it felt more like I was dragging her instead of leading her. When I dared a glance over my shoulder, I could see two of those things closing in fast. I yanked hard on her arm, causing her to cry out, but a little pain was the least of my concerns. If we didn't put enough distance between us and them, we'd be dead before we got to the store.

As for the others, I could see Irene speeding along ahead of me, but I'd lost track of everyone else. I just hoped that they were alright.

"How are we gonna keep these things out once we get there?!" I called out to Irene, my heart pounding in my chest.

"I used to work there! I know how the gate works."

"No! NO!!"

The yell came from behind us, and I turned to look again. Alex and Sarah had been cornered, and the two chasing us had become distracted by the noise. It was a perfect opportunity to put more distance between us, if I just kept running.

But I didn't keep running. I stopped, the saleswoman bumping into me as I stood and watched. If I did nothing, Alex and Sarah would die. Hell, even if I tried to help they'd probably still die, and me along with them. I'd been in two encounters with these things already, and I felt like I was pushing my luck. But, watching them, I knew that if I kept running I'd hate myself for the rest of my life, however long or short that happened to be.

"You've got to keep going. Don't look back." I looked the woman in the eyes and pushed her towards the sporting

goods store, hoping she had enough of her faculties left to understand me and keep on moving. She looked at me for a moment with those big watery eyes, then turned away. At first I
thought she was just going to collapse into herself again, but
she took off running. Good. One less thing to worry about.

Focusing fully on Alex and Sarah, I could see there
were four of those things closing in. I started to regret my self-
less act; I had no weapon and no plan. Sarah kept screaming
whenever one got close, and Alex was doing a poor job of keeping them at bay. However, instead of focusing on him, the one
who was striking at them, they all seemed focused on Sarah. It
made no sense. *Unless*?

Taking a deep breath, I yelled as loudly as I could.
"HEY! FUCKERS! OVER HERE!"

All four turned and began to make their way towards
me. They didn't make it more than five feet before Sarah fell to
her knees, a blubbering mess. It was recapturing their attention.

Sound was the key. I had no idea why, but it was clearly
what motivated them.

"Get her to be quiet! I'll try and lead them away!"
Christ, why was I suddenly acting the hero? I didn't even know
these people forty minutes ago, and now here I was risking my
life to save them. "HEY! BACK TO ME YOU WALKING
PIECES OF SHIT!"

I kicked repeatedly at a nearby garbage can, the metal
clang echoing in the nearly empty mall. It got the attention of
the Shushers again, and this time my antics were loud enough
that any noise Sarah might still be making wasn't important;
now I was the one who needed to be silenced.

Once they were close enough that I was confident they
wouldn't become distracted again, I ran past them, back the
way we had come: Hannigan's. There were probably more of
those things in there, but since they were attracted to noise,
maybe I could find a way to lose them once I was inside. I still
had no idea where Charles or Shawn had gone, but when I
looked over my shoulder both Sarah and Alex were running towards the sports store. At least they escaped. My mind was going a mile a minute as I tried to think my way out of the mess
I'd gotten into.

I took the corner too quickly, stumbling and nearly wiping out. Thankfully the entrance to Hannigan's was empty, devoid of more of those things. I made a beeline inside, and wondered if I could close the doors in time to keep them out, but it was no use. Hannigan's lacked a gate like the other, smaller stores had, and every door was not only made of glass, but required a key to lock. Cursing my luck, I dashed for the escalator.

It was still functioning, and I got a slight sense of vertigo as I bounded up the steps, two at a time. The feeling of disorientation was enough to cause me to trip and fall flat on my face as I reached the summit of my climb.

Crawling quickly across the floor, I was able to get behind a cell phone display case as the first Shusher reached the top. I held my breath and watched. The other three were nowhere to be seen, but that didn't mean they weren't still somewhere in the store. I just hoped they hadn't given up the chase and gone after the others. Then my *heroic sacrifice* would have been in vain.

It was looking from side to side, scanning the entire area. I realized that it wasn't using its eyes, but turning its head so that the holes where the ears would be could pick up sound. More proof these things could only hear and not see.

I reached, carefully, into my pocket and pulled out my wallet: driver's license, a few credit cards, and several pictures. All easily replaced. I drew back and threw it, as hard as I could, deeper into the store. When I heard a thunk, followed by a loud crash and the sound of glass breaking, it was like sweet music to my ears.

The Shusher jerked its head towards where the sound had come from, raised its finger to its mouth, and took off running. Not wanting to risk it hearing me leave my hiding spot, I waited for a count of ten before I crept out.

It was deathly quiet in the store, and it felt like I was home free. I let out the breath I'd been holding in, slowly and quietly. These things used to be people, and something was causing them to move after death. They tracked by sound, and were so preoccupied by it that they would ignore you if you were quiet enough.

I looked at the escalator, wondering if I should try heading back to the entrance. I couldn't immediately see a down escalator, which meant that it would take longer, either to find the down escalator or fight my way back down the one I came up on. There was also no way to know if the noise I made walking on the metal steps would give away my location.

On the other hand, there was only one of them up here with me as far as I knew, and he was too busy trying to figure out what had caused that crash. I *could* take my time and be as silent as possible while I looked for the down escalator, or even an elevator.

Looking around for any sign of the things, I closed my eyes, said a prayer to whoever might be listening, and made my way in the opposite direction from where the Shusher had gone, deeper into the second floor. If I was lucky I was also going the in the direction to get out of this place and regroup with the others.

After a few minutes of walking, I was starting to get annoyed. Most stores had *something* pointing customers to their desired destinations. In Hannigan's, however, there wasn't so much as a sign over each department. It was infuriating. I breathed a sigh of relief when I finally located a standing map near housewares.

A big red dot showed my location, and the down escalator was closer than I thought. The only problem was, it pointed towards the street entrance of the store, which meant more of a chance I'd run into the other Shushers on the ground floor as I made my way back into the mall.

Scanning the map again, I saw an elevator near the bathrooms, but it was also near where I threw my wallet. It would be a risk, but it was also right near the mall entrance and would let me make a quick escape.

Standing out in the open was beginning to make me feel exposed and vulnerable, so I headed towards the down escalator. The elevator may have seemed safer, but if the Shushers were waiting when I got off, it would be an inescapable death trap.

I ducked down an aisle of dishware, and moved along it as quickly and quietly as I could, ducking to keep my head below the top of the shelf. I was so preoccupied with looking over my shoulder, I wasn't paying attention as I exited the aisle and turned left, running into something solid. Thinking I had just bumped into the Shusher that I had tried to avoid earlier, I let out a gasp and stumbled backwards. My elbow struck a display of dinnerware, knocking several plates to the floor where they shattered on impact.

"Quiet!! Yer gonna let them all know we're in here!!"

I never figured I'd be so happy to see two people I barely knew. Charles, who I had bumped into, was rubbing his arm as Shawn continued to chastise me. "There's no fucking way they didn't hear that! We're fucking dead!"

It seemed pointless to apologize, so I just shrugged as I moved past the two and into the open walkway. "Maybe we could all still make the escalator before they...You've gotta be fucking kidding me!!" I couldn't help but cry out as I saw two of the Shushers come up the escalator, fighting against the downward motion of the steps.

If I hadn't been about to piss myself in terror, I'd have found it comical. They were just moving so...*slow*. Each step forward almost sent them two back.

"There's a service area in the back!" Charles pushed past me, and I followed, trusting that he knew where he was going.

I didn't look behind us. I just hoped those things remained preoccupied with their ascent up the stairs and would soon forget about us. Within a few moments we were at a set of sturdy double doors behind a sales counter. Charles pulled on the handle, but it didn't budge.

"What...they never lock these!" He sounded surprised.

"How do you know about this if you don't work here?"

Charles blushed slightly at my question and shrugged. "*I* don't work here, but, uh...*Darcie* does. This is the only area without security cameras and where we can...indulge in each other.

I furrowed my brow at him, more surprised than uncomfortable. The man looked like he was pushing sixty, and was certainly not the kind of person I would have pictured sneaking away for some afternoon delight in the back room of a busy department store. He banged on the doors and tried them again, cursing loudly.

"Quiet, man! They're gonna come for us!!" Shawn's voice was filled with panic.

"They already know we're here! Anything we do now won't flippin' matter."

Things weren't looking good. If the Shushers caught us here, we were as good as dead. "Are you sure anyone is even *in* there?"

"Of course I am! She said she'd meet me after work tonight!"

"Charles?" The voice from the other side was muffled, but I could tell it was calling out his name.

"Yeah, he's here! You have to let us in, please!!" Shawn yelled out

Charles' began to bang the door harder, calling out, "Darcie?! It's me! Open up, sugartits!!"

Shawn and I exchanged a look, but I had nothing to say. If we survived this, I had a lot of questions for Charles.

"How do I know it's you and not one of those dead people?"

"Who else knows how you like yer pussy licked, baby?"

"Charles, this isn't the time!" I yelled as I saw two Shushers come into view. That still left two unaccounted for, and I didn't want to be surprised by their sudden appearance while I was on the wrong side of a locked door.

"Oh, you horny old goat!" The doors unlocked, but we didn't wait before we shoved our way through, nearly knocking a young and attractive woman down in the process.

I slammed the doors shut, turning the deadbolt just as the Shushers started to pound on them. I looked around for Darcie, and was surprised when I realized the young woman in front of me *was* Darcie.

I had a *lot* of questions for Charles.

VI

I was relieved that the area we found ourselves in was-n't a dead end. It seemed to be some sort of servicing depart-ment, probably for repairing electronics and small appliances in-house. There were two separate doors on the back wall, one with a red 'EXIT' sign above it.

I put my finger to my lips in an effort to get everyone to remain quiet, hoping that the Shushers banging on the door would forget about us and move on if we were silent. After thirty or forty agonizing seconds the pounding slowed, and then finally stopped. It was another five seconds before I let out the breath I hadn't realized I'd been holding.

Looking over at the others, I was shocked to see Charles and Darcie in a deep embrace, lips and tongues mov-ing wildly. Sure, I wanted them to be quiet, but I hardly meant *that*.

"Oh god, baby, I thought you were dead!"

"I'm just glad you're alright, Daddy."

I cringed inwardly at the display, but we had more im-portant things to worry about than these two making out like high schoolers. I turned to Shawn. "How did you two end up here?"

"Charles ran back to Hannigan's when those things cor-nered Sarah and Alex." Shawn hung his head, biting his lip. "I was too scared to try and help, so I just followed after him."

"You're what, sixteen?" I asked.

"Eighteen," Shawn replied with an annoyed, defensive tone.

"Sorry, eighteen. None of us have ever experienced anything like this. Running *away* from danger isn't anything to be ashamed of. Hell, under normal circumstances I would've done the same thing. I don't like confrontation." I did my best to reassure him, hoping he would feel better about the predicament we found ourselves in.

It wouldn't do anyone any good to second guess themselves, or to beat themselves up over things they did or did not do. But thinking about that made me remember my own actions, particularly moving to save Alex and Sarah, and I had to lean against a workbench as my legs started to shake.

"Jesus. I almost died." The words escaped my lips as barely a whisper. It wasn't just saving those two, either. I kept getting myself into these dangerous situations, and escaping by the skin of my teeth. It was only a matter of time before my luck gave out and I ended up like one of the Shushers.

I turned to look at Charles and Darcie. Trauma and terror must be powerful aphrodisiacs, because his hand was now up her shirt and her hands were straying dangerously close to his waistband.

"Can you two knock it off? You can fuck when we get the hell out of here." I did little to hide my disgust at how the two of them were carrying on. On one hand I could understand, and even appreciate it. On the other, get a goddamn room.

"Uh...yeah, sure..." Darcie sheepishly replied and smoothed out her shirt.

Charles looked aggravated that I had interrupted his makeout session, and raised his voice at me. "I can fuck whenever I want, you little pissant!"

His eyes went wide as soon as he said the last word, realizing what he had done. The banging on the double doors resumed, much more frenzied now.

"We need to get out of here, fast." Turning to Darcie I asked, "Do you know a way we can get to Sports 'N Stuff from here?"

She shook her head. "No, at least I don't think..." Her voice trailed off and then her eyes went wide as she remembered something. "There's a freight elevator that goes down to the basement, and I think there's a service tunnel that connects with the rest of the mall! It's just in the hallway in the back." She pointed towards the door with the exit sign.

The thought of going deeper into the bowels of this place was far from appealing, but we didn't have much of a choice. If all four of those things were banging on the doors, there was no telling how long they would actually hold. The only thought that gave me comfort was that these things could-n't come to life unless there was a dead body for them to poss-es. There couldn't have been *that* many people still stuck in the mall, right?

Moving past Darcie, I headed towards the door she had pointed to. I was about to open it when I thought I heard nois-es coming from the other side. I pressed my ear against the door, and there was a distinct sound of rattling metal. I sud-denly felt claustrophobic and trapped.

"Christ. I think there's one back here, too."

Darcie frowned, and worry filled her eyes. "There was-n't five minutes ago!"

"Is this door the only way to the elevator, hun?" Charles asked.

"Yeah. The other door is just a closet."

Fucking hell. There was no other way out; we'd have to fight.

"What if we arm ourselves, let it in, and then attack it?" Shawn made his way towards the closet, opening it up. He ri-fled through it, looking for anything we could utilize as weapons.

"You saw what happened when that one guy's kid at-tacked my...friend. He nearly destroyed its fucking head and it *still* managed to keep going." Charles sounded worried. "How the hell are we gonna stop these things if they don't need a head?!"

I tried not to think about that. Ignoring the constant banging coming from the double doors, I joined Shawn in looking through the closet. It was mostly empty, save a few brooms and dustpans, some circuit boards, and dozens of spools of wire. It was hardly an inspiring assortment. Cursing under my breath, I grabbed the two brooms and started to un-screw the brushes from the handles. At least they were made from solid wood.

Charles came up behind me, and I looked over my shoulder at him. He seemed capable enough, but I wondered if he had the strength to attack one of those things without getting himself hurt.

"No offense, but I think Shawn and I can handle this. You get the door, and if you see an opening, make a break for it with Darcie." Turning to Shawn, I continued. "We're not going to try and kill it. We just gotta make it come into the room to get us, and then try and trap it in here so we can all make it to the elevator. Got it?"

Shawn nodded his understanding and I took a few short breaths to mentally prepare myself. When the hell had I become a hero? My gut started to quake, and I suddenly felt nauseous. It was hard to believe there was anything left in my stomach after vomiting earlier.

As Charles moved into position under the exit sign, I turned and violently retched in front of the workbench, heaving so hard I thought my eyes were going to burst. I felt something thick and viscous pour from my mouth. Seconds passed, but it felt like an eternity before it was done.

After the ordeal was over, I dared to look down, then coughed and choked as I backed away. Whatever I had just vomited up was pitch black and *moving on its own.*

"Th...the fuck is *that*?!"

I couldn't even register who was speaking; I was too transfixed by whatever the hell this thing was that had just come *out* of me. It moved for a few more seconds, and then lay still. I finally shook myself out of the stupor I was in and poked at the blob with my broom handle. It gave no further signs of movement.

I looked at the others, and each of them had a look of horror and disgust on their face. Had the situation been reversed, I probably would have reacted the same way. The only explanation that came to mind was that I had been outside with the security guard. Was that blackness surrounding the mall toxic? Had I breathed it in or ingested it somehow?

I noticed that the banging was getting louder and more insistent now that I had vomited. Was it somehow connected? I didn't care. I just wanted out of that room, that store, that *goddamn mall* more than ever.

I looked right at Charles and spat out, "Open the fucking door."

He stood there, staring at me, as I white-knuckled the broom handle. For a second I thought he wouldn't, but he turned and put one hand on the deadbolt, and the other on the knob. Turning to Shawn, he began to mouth a countdown. When he got to one, he unlocked the door and threw it open.

Everything was frozen in time. As soon as the door was open every muscle in my body tensed up. I was ready to strike at anything that came through the door, but the seconds stretched out and nothing happened. I took a step forward, the only one who dared to inspect past the door.

There was nothing. The hallway went forward about fifteen or twenty feet, then turned to the right. I didn't let myself relax; I couldn't see beyond the corner. I didn't want to get killed because I was careless at the wrong moment, so I slowly crept forward to inspect further.

Shawn, on the other hand, wasn't as cautious. "Alright, let's get the fuck outta here!" He darted into the hallway, and before anyone could stop him he was turning the corner and was out of sight. Charles and Darcie followed quickly after, and I stood there, wondering if I was the only one that remembered there was possibly something still out there.

Before I left the room, I took a minute to glance back down at the pile of black sludge that I had vomited up. A gasp escaped my lips when I saw that it was gone. The vomit and bile were still there, staining the floor, but the black goop was missing. I jerked my head around, trying not to panic as I wondered where it could have gone, or if it had just been my imagination.

"Fuck this."

I immediately abandoned my search, leaving the room, and slamming the door shut behind me. I caught up with the others at the freight elevator, but it was surprising that we hadn't encountered anything in the hallway.

Darcie was fiddling with a key ring, trying to find the right key to unlock the elevator gate, so I took a moment to look around. There was a chain link door at the end of the hallway; I assumed it led to the roof access. I wandered over to check it, and it was firmly locked. Nothing could have gotten through. *What the hell had I been making the noise I heard?*

Darcie was still searching for the right key when I heard another strange sound. It reminded me of high grit sandpaper rubbing against wood. A steady, rhythmic 'shua' sound. I turned towards where it was coming from, and couldn't believe what I was seeing. A splotch of black was moving along the floor, right towards us. It had to be whatever I threw up.

"Oh my god..." Charles uttered behind me. "It's the shit that came outta David!"

We had nothing adequate to fight it off with. The whole thing appeared to be liquid, changing its shape and form randomly as it inched towards us, and I doubted that a broom handle would do much to stop it. I heard the familiar click of a padlock unlocking, then the clattering of a keyring hitting the floor. There was a screech as the large metal grate slid upwards, and footsteps as everyone ran inside.

Part of me didn't want to take my eyes off the thing, now on the wall, but I turned to join the others. All three were inside the elevator already, and I saw something move on the other side of the locked gate at the end of the hallway.

Whatever it was, it appeared to be the same material as the black spot, only much, much more of it. It was shiny, too, like an oil slick. *What the hell is this stuff?* I thought, doing my best not to freak out over the fact that some of the stuff had been *inside* me. I didn't want to wait around for answers, though.

I was moving towards the elevator, when Charles brought the gate down right in front of me. His face was unreadable, but I knew exactly what was going on.

"Let me in! There's more of that black stuff coming!"

"It came *out* of you! How do we know you aren't gonna turn into some kind of fucking monster, like those skinless freaks?!"

There was true fear in his words, and I had to admit that he was right; there was no way to be sure. I just knew I didn't want to die in that goddamn hallway. "Please, Charles. You gotta let me in. It's gonna kill me if it gets here."

He looked like he was debating what he should do when Darcie slammed her hand on a floor button. While Charles' face was furrowed with conflicting emotions, she had smug satisfaction painted on hers. *That bitch.* I frowned as I watched the main elevator doors close and heard the motor sputter to life.

The ooze on the wall shot past me and headed towards the larger mass. I watched in fascination as it was readily absorbed into the bulk. Maybe what had been inside me was just part of a larger whole, seeking to rejoin itself.

I didn't have much time to ponder, as the black slime started to push itself through the chain link door, oozing through the holes. Watching it reminded me of watching meat go through a grinder, or modeling clay through a toy extruder. Thick, gooey strings of it leaked through, and rejoined on the other side; my side. Back in the service area, I could hear the double doors the Shushers had been banging against finally give way and break open.

I was trapped.

VII

My mind raced. There was no way in hell I could get past two Shushers in such close quarters, and there was no telling what sort of creature that black gunk was, or if it could be harmed. I was wondering if it was possible to surprise them before they came around the corner, when a glint on the floor caught my eye. Darcie had dropped her keys. There *had* to be one for that locked gate.

The sludge had finished pushing its way through, and was making its slow and steady way towards me. I quickly grabbed the keys, pressed my back against the wall, and shimmied past it, being careful not to let it touch me.

Thankfully, it seemed far more interested in the elevator; it was heading straight for the closed doors. I took my eyes off of it, hesitantly, and looked at the keyring, trying not to let anxiety and fear cloud my judgement and force me to make a costly mistake.

There were twelve keys on the ring. One was for the elevator gate, and two others looked far too large for the small keyhole. Three more looked to be far too small. This left six possible keys. Picking one at random, I tried it in the lock. It didn't work, and the jingle of keys sent a shiver down my spine as it was answered by a 'shhh' noise. Daring to glance over my shoulder, I could see them, at the far end of the hallway, doing that fucking awful shushing motion with their bloody, skinless fingers pressed against their non-existent lips.

I'm not fucking dying here.

I kept trying key after key, cursing at each wrong choice, as footsteps echoed through the hall. I didn't dare look back and just kept trying until I got to the last key. *Just my luck*, I thought, as the gate sprung open. I quickly jumped through, slammed it shut behind me, and locked it again.

The Shushers slammed into the chain-link door, splattering my face and chest with blood. They both backed up, and ran at it again. When that failed to work, they tried to open it like a regular door, but it remained locked. Confident that it would hold for the time being, I let my guard down slightly and began watching the black goo.

It was piled in front of the elevator door, and it appeared to be getting smaller. It took me a few seconds of watching to realize that it wasn't shrinking, but seeping through the cracks of the door, and into the elevator shaft. Even though Darcie had made the decision to leave me to die, I hoped at least Charles and Shawn were off the elevator by the time the thing made its way towards them. As the last bit of it slipped from view, I turned away from the two Shushers banging on the door and towards what was left of the hallway that was behind the locked door.

There wasn't much to the area, unfortunately. It was dark and there were no other entrances, only a ladder leading up; I assumed it was the roof access. I looked back the way I had come. There was no way in hell I was going to backtrack, so up was my only option.

When I got to the top I let out a sigh of relief; there was a slot for a padlock, but the lock was missing. I unfastened the hatch and pushed against it, but met a surprising amount of resistance. I pushed again with more force, grunting a bit as I exerted all my strength. A pitch-black sky greeted me as it finally swung open.

I hoisted myself out onto the roof, and looked around. There were safety lights around the edge, and track lights every five feet or so, but they gave off so little light they were practically worthless. I was alone on the rooftop, so I made my way towards the closest edge and looked over.

The mall was still surrounded by the void, and it looked like the unaffected area I had noticed before had gotten smaller. Trying to focus on the darkness made my head spin and my brain itch, so I looked away. It was pointless. None of this made any goddamn sense, and I was still trapped.

I looked around the rooftop itself; there was a small structure with a door, and a ladder off one side leading to the lower roof that was the rest of the mall. I made my way towards the ladder, hoping to find a way back inside, even though I knew the chances of another access point being unlocked were slim. However, when I looked over the edge I was overwhelmed with a sense of vertigo and had to step back. Maybe going down that way was a bad idea.

I was moving to try the door when I noticed that the hatch I had come through was not resting flat against the roof. I thought back to how difficult the hatch had been to open, and was dreading what could possibly be underneath it. I made my way back to it, cautiously, and used the toe of my shoe to kick it closed, exposing what was underneath,

I gasped. It was a body, or, more accurately, a skeleton. Nearly every bit of flesh was gone, and most of it was covered in a slick, black residue that reminded me of the sludge creature from before. The same stuff I had thrown up.

I leaned in a bit closer, and saw that a majority of the stuff was covering the *interior* side of the bones. It had come from inside this poor bastard. Looking at the skull, I saw nothing near the mouth or on the teeth. Maybe my sensitive stomach had actually saved my life. I still didn't know where the stuff had come from or how it ended up inside me, but seeing the mouth clean of it gave me a small measure of comfort that I wasn't going to die.

Taking a breath, I headed back to the door, and tried it. I wasn't sure what I was expecting, but I was happily surprised when it opened. I peered into the dark and saw the thin outline of a stairway leading downward. There was nothing for me here on the roof, or back down the hatch, so I had little choice but to brave the darkness.

Before moving forward, I turned to look back at the sky. It reminded me of a moonless night, only instead of stars, it was a plain black canvas. The whole thing was unnerving, and I didn't linger. When I turned back to the stairs, I was filled with a sudden desire to figure out what was going on, and to try and reverse it. My thoughts also drifted to the sales woman, and I hoped she was alright. I even hoped the bastards in the elevator made it out okay. I couldn't yell at them if they were dead.

I began to descend the stairway, but with no light to see I missed a step. I tumbled into the darkness. My body fell against the stairs, rolling downward until my head made contact with the wall at the bottom and I immediately lost consciousness.

*****

Sunday. After church. My mother always forced me to go. We were a good Christian family, and good Christian folk went to church on Sunday. Only heathens and sinners stayed home to watch TV or play outside. I wanted to throw off the itchy, wool blazer she made me wear. Wanted to throw it off and run through a field barefoot.

No, not run, *fly*. I wanted to fly like a bird and soar through the air, the blue sky at my back and the green grass beneath me. Moving so fast it all seemed a beautiful green blur. It was magnificent. *I* was magnificent.

Yes, the black sky at my back, as a sea of red splayed out in every direction underneath me. I flapped my wings made of bone and heard the powerful dirge of the dead god in the distance. I was losing altitude, fast, but it didn't matter. I welcomed becoming one with the crimson god, to give my flesh in tribute to his dark desires.

He wanted so much flesh. For what I did not know. I didn't care. I wanted to tear it off in strips, gladly, to please him. Gouge my eyes from my skull so I could only see what he let me. My blood would become his.

Mother would be so proud of her baby boy.

*****

I woke with a start, my head and neck at an unusual, uncomfortable angle in relation to the rest of my body. My joints felt stiff and painful as I moved from my prone position on the floor. There was no way to know how long I had been out, but I immediately sensed I wasn't alone.

"Who...who's there?"

If it was a Shusher, or more sludge, I'd be dead anyway. It was as dark in the stairway as the sky outside, so I wouldn't even see it coming. I was about to ask again, starting to doubt my senses, when a bright flash of light in my face blinded me.

"Gahh!!"

"You have your eyes still. Good. Thought you'd become one of those skinless freaks."

"You have me at a disadvantage."

I continued to get up from the floor, rubbing my neck as I tried to look past the light. It was some sort of high-powered flashlight. It stayed trained on me as the female voice continued, ignoring my implied question.

"What were you doing on the roof?"

Turning away from the light and rubbing my sore eyes, I debated telling her the whole story. Would she think I was crazy? Then again, I couldn't think of any valid reason to keep things from her, so I spilled everything; from the encounter with the security guard to when she found me. I kept the dream to myself, though.

"I didn't need a whole recap, just what you were doing the roof." The way she spoke was odd. As if she were dancing around something only she knew about, and was trying to avoid telling me directly. "How long has it been?"

"How long?" I asked. "Since this all began...I'd guess a few hours. Three at most...though I have no clue how long I was out on the stairs."

"Fuck. *Fuck*."

Her voice sounded familiar. I couldn't place it exactly because of the echo from the empty stairwell, but there was no denying the feeling that I knew it.

"What is it?"

The light moved downward, and I could finally start to see her features. "It hasn't been a few hours. It's been almost two days."

As my eyes adjusted to the light and darkness I could see her more and more clearly. They went wide as I recognized her: it was the sales woman. She looked like she'd been through hell and back.

"You mean to tell me I was passed out on these stairs for almost two days?!"

"I don't know."

"That doesn't make any sense. There's no *way* it could have been two days."

She looked pensive. "Shawn and Darcie said you got split up in Hannigan's, and when you didn't come back we figured you were either dead or one of the things."

"Well, I'm not. Charles and Darcie shut the elevator door on me and left me for dead. I'm going to have words with all three of them once we get back."

The sales woman remained silent, and looked away from me, rubbing her arm.

"What is it?"

"Charles is dead. So's Emeline." Her voice faded and her face took on a thousand yard stare. I wanted to pry, to ask what happened to them, but I didn't want to risk her withdrawing into herself again like she had when all this had begun.

"Hey, where are the others? Still at the sports place?"

She blinked several times, shaking her head slightly before answering me. "No, we're actually just below. We managed to find a place near the food court. When we heard the commotion I drew the short straw to check it out."

"Wait, we're not still above Hannigan's?"

She looked confused. "No, of course not. This is the roof access from the mall service tunnel behind the restaurants."

"But...nevermind." I sighed and focused on the more important issue. "I thought you said it had been almost two days. I was *just* separated from Charles, Shawn and Darcie about fifteen minutes before my fall."

"You say it's been minutes, but I know it's been days. Emeline exploded and killed Charles yesterday. *Yesterday!*" She bit her lower lip. "None of this makes any sense."

I could only stare at her as she spoke, her lip trembling.

"We'll figure it out. Maybe I hit my head harder than I thought."

She seemed to accept this answer. Whether it was because she didn't want to keep standing around in a dark stairwell thinking about it, or because she actually believed me, I couldn't tell.

"Okay. Like I said, we're just below. Follow me."

She aimed the flashlight down the stairs, and I complied. Somehow I had lost track of almost forty-eight hours. Was it being outside the mall? Did time somehow pass faster out there? *Goddammit*, my head hurt.

VIII

The trip back to the hideout behind the food court was uneventful. The quiet made me increasingly paranoid that something was going to jump out and try and kill us. By the time we got there I was covered in a cold sweat.

The safe zone itself was a series of small service and storage areas behind a few of the restaurants, all connected by an access hallway. The saleswoman, whose name, I found out, was Victoria King, explained that they had picked the area precisely *because* it only had the one entrance. Less chance of something being able to sneak up on them without their realizing it. To me it felt like a death trap.

At the door, she knocked twice, waited five seconds, then knocked four times. I could hear the sound of something heavy being pushed away from the door and it opened a second later. Shawn looked like he'd seen a ghost as Victoria and I pushed past him and into the room.

Inside, I saw Darcie, Irene, Alex and Sarah. I looked at Darcie, but she avoided my gaze. I frowned; their decision to leave me was still fresh in my mind. Glancing around the area, I was surprised by how sizable it was. There was more than enough room for everyone to have their own separate corner carved out. Dozens of boxes of nonperishable food lined the walls. At least we wouldn't starve before this was over. Assuming it ever actually ended.

"Holy fuck. You're actually alive."

Irene wheeled over to me, giving me a once over with her eyes. I smiled meekly at her as Alex and Sarah came rushing over.

"We...we never thought we'd get a chance to say thank you. If you hadn't...well, there's no way we'd be alive now," Alex said, before pulling me in for a hug.

I was never one for personal contact. Even handshakes tend to put me on edge, so I awkwardly patted his back and rode it out until the embrace was through. Shawn was standing next to Sarah, and the look of shock was still plastered on his face. I wouldn't be surprised if it stayed that way permanently.

"What the hell happened? How did you get out?!" he asked

I relayed my tale, glossing over how I had been left behind. There was shame in Shawn's eyes, and Darcie avoided looking at me while I spoke. Instead she busied herself with something near her bedroll. When I got to the part about the roof, I left out the dream as well. I finished my story when Victoria found me in the stairwell.

"I wouldn't stand too close to him. He's bound to go like Emeline did."

All eyes turned to Darcie. I realized I had never asked what happened.

"What *did* happen with her and Charles? And why do you think I'm going to do the same?"

Shawn bit his lip, and looked like he was going to answer my question but Darcie jumped up and stormed over to me, pointing an accusing finger. "Why didn't you tell them about how you puked up all that black shit? The same black shit Emeline got all over Charles when the fucking bitch went suicide bomber!!"

I could feel the color draining from my face. "W...what?"

"Don't try and fucking hide it. You're infected, or sick, or part of this or whatever the fuck she was. You puked it, but she..." Tears started to well up in her eyes and she couldn't finish her sentence. I reached out a hand to try and comfort her, but she slapped it away. "If you all are smart, you'll throw his ass back out there. He was as good as dead but now he's standing here, *two fucking days later*, without so much as a goddamn scratch. It ain't right. It ain't fucking right."

They all just stared at me, and even Victoria had started to inch away. I took a step back so I could see everyone. "Someone tell me exactly what happened with Emeline and Charles."

Irene shrugged. "We got to the sports store, but for some reason the gate wasn't working. Alex, Sarah, and Victoria met up with me and Emeline there, and we grabbed a few bats and some other gear we thought would be helpful, and just ran. We had no idea where the hell we were going to go, but we decided to try the food court. At the very least, we figured we could get some food supplies, water, that sort of thing. It was dumb luck we found this place." She motioned around the area.

"That's great, but, *what happened?*" I pressed.

Everyone started to look uncomfortable, but Irene continued. "About an hour or two later, we heard some commotion outside. It was Shawn, Darcie and Charles, all dealing with a Shusher. They had caught the attention of one while they were foraging for food, but they'd managed to kill it. We all decided to hole up here until we could figure out a plan. David, according to them, you were dead."

She glared over at Darcie, who just frowned and turned away. "They told us they watched you die, so we took it at face value. If we had known, maybe we could have helped you."

"No. There was nothing you could have done. It's suicide to be out there for long, and there's no telling where I could have been. You did the right thing."

Irene's face eased at my words and she gave me a half smile. "Maybe. Anyway, yesterday we were moving stuff around in here, trying to make it more comfortable, taking stock of our supplies, talking about making another run to the sporting goods store for weapons, camping stuff, whatever, when Emeline started to complain that her stomach hurt."

"We all thought she just needed a minute, so while we were moving things in here, Charles and Darcie kept her company in the hallway," Shawn added.

Irene nodded. "When she started to moan I went out there to try and get her to be quiet. Ten seconds later she was gripping her stomach and crying out, loud. Charles moved to try and cover her mouth or something when she...burst."

"She *exploded*?" I was dumbfounded.

"Well, her stomach ruptured, and this black stuff came pouring out. She was dead within seconds, and it covered Charles just as quickly." Irene wheeled past me, opened the door, and headed out. I followed and saw her pointing to a dark patch on the floor. I was surprised I had missed it when I first arrived.

"Whatever it was, he didn't suffer long. He was gone within seconds. The black stuff just...absorbed them both. Before we could react, it was gone."

I stared at the dark area for the longest time. I could faintly make out the outline of a body. Maybe it was a trick of the light. Maybe I was trying too hard to see something that wasn't there. Either way, I turned and we headed back into the room. Once inside, Shawn started to push the shelf back in front of the door when Darcie started to yell.

"You are NOT locking me in here with that...thing! He tried to kill us once, and he'll do it again!"

"Darcie, what are you talking about?" Alex asked.

"I told you! He puked up the same shit that killed Emeline and Charles! It tried to kill us, and then when we found more of it and ditched his ass, he makes it out alive?!"

"You *what*?" Irene angrily wheeled over to Darcie. "You said you had no choice but to leave him behind. Now you're saying you ditched him?"

"Fuck you, cripple. He's fine! Except he's not...that fucker is gonna kill us."

I took a short breath and decided to take culpability. "I did puke something up, but I have no idea what, or why. It was the same black stuff we encountered trying to escape, and it sounds like the same stuff that killed the other two."

"Well, you didn't explode, and you're still standing after two days. For all we know *everyone* is probably gonna puke that shit up." Irene never took her eyes off Darcie. "I know you were scared, but leaving him was a dick thing to do."

She turned in her wheelchair, and Darcie yelped in pain. Irene had run over her foot. The smirk on her face told me it wasn't an accident.

"David, there's another storage room down the hall from here. It's got food and some bottles of water. You okay with staying there, just for now?" She looked at me, trying her best to hide the fear in her eyes.

I nodded, knowing that arguing was only going to work everyone into a panic, or worse. Once I spent a night or two on my own to prove I was fine, I was sure the group would accept me again. With the way Darcie continued to eye me, being somewhere else was actually something of a relief. If I stayed, I just knew that she would do something stupid, or she'd force me to do something I'd regret.

"Yeah. I'll be fine."

"The knock Victoria used to get in is the way we'll know you're...you. If you need something just let us know."

After Irene finished speaking, everyone looked at me expectantly. *Ah, you expect me to leave right* now. Fine. I'd prove to them I was fine and then we could work together to get out of this hellhole.

"I'm going with David." Victoria's declaration surprised me.

"Are you sure that's wise?" Alex asked. A few minutes ago he was thanking me for saving his life and hugging me like a brother. Now he was standing between Sarah and me like I was a strange dog he didn't trust.

"I'll be fine. He saved my life," Victoria emphasized the word life as she looked right at Alex, "so I feel I owe him this much. Plus, I can keep an eye on him and if I need to, I'll kill him."

That last part didn't fill me with much confidence but we made our way back out into the hall, the sound of the shelf sliding into place behind us.

"Kill me, huh?"

She shrugged. "Only as a last resort. I figure if you were going to be dangerous, it would have happened already. Also, I wanted to get away from Shawn. The way he's been looking at me is creepy."

I nodded as we made our way down the hall. I opened the door to the other storage room; it was about the half size of the last one, but the shelves were lined with just as many boxes.

"Ever wonder why the power's still on?" Victoria pointed towards the lights.

"No. If I start to wonder that, knowing my luck, they'll shut off." The overhead lights flickered as if on cue, but they remained on. "See?!" I joked.

Victoria smiled, but it was grim and there was no real amusement behind it. She motioned over towards one corner of the room. "I'll make myself a spot over here, by the door, and you can take one of the corners by the far wall."

She may have believed I wasn't a danger, but she still took a spot near the door. Given the circumstances, it was smart. She also didn't insist we move a shelf in front of the door. If I *did* turn out to be something dangerous, at least she could get out quickly. I didn't mention my observations as I made myself a place to sleep.

"Have you thought any more about how you lost two days?"

I shook my head as I moved some items around to fashion a makeshift bed. "Not really. The only thing I can think of is that it had something to do with me being outside. Either time moves much slower out there, or I just blacked out and didn't realize it."

I looked over at her when she didn't reply, and saw that she was dozing, sitting on the floor with her back against the wall. She must have been exhausted. I decided to let her sleep and I got onto my crudely fashioned cot and stared up at the ceiling lights.

Two days. And there was that dream, too. I closed my eyes, praying I didn't have anymore like it.

IX

I awoke with a start, and for one brief, glorious moment I forgot where I was and what was happening. But it all came crashing back as soon as the room around me came into focus. I frowned, sighing deeply to myself. Standing, a wave of dizziness washed over me and I had to reach for a nearby shelf for support. In my effort to keep from falling, I knocked something over and it hit the ground with a dull thud. Victoria stirred, but didn't wake.

The overhead light was dim, but bright enough that I could make out what had fallen. It was a bag of powdered sugar. I knelt down and picked it up, placing it back on the shelf. Looking around, I saw that almost every item in here was something related to baking. There was nothing in our food stores that could be eaten without extensive cooking and preparation.

That was when I realized...I wasn't hungry. The events of the past days had been stressful enough to suppress anybody's appetite, but if I had really been passed out upstairs for more than a day I should be famished. But as I looked around the room I felt nothing more than a slight nausea. Was there more of that sludge inside of me? Was I going to explode like Emeline had?

Worrying about my impending death wasn't helpful. Either I would find a way out of this hell, or I'd die. Letting myself fret was only making me anxious. Instead I started to dig through the shelves and boxes more thoroughly, in an effort to find either more substantial foodstuffs or some kind of equipment that could be used as a weapon.

Satisfied that I had explored everything the shelf in front of me had to offer, I turned to the next one and noticed Victoria was sitting up, watching me. When had she woken up? And why hadn't she said anything?

"Morning. Or night. I'm not sure which anymore."

She continued to stare at me, and then yawned. "Does it matter? I can't even tell how long I was asleep."

"Same." I didn't feel exhausted anymore, but I also didn't feel rested. I couldn't have gotten more than a few scant hours of sleep.

"What are you doing?"

"Looking for food or supplies. Anything that might give us a hand here."

She got up and joined me in the search. Irene had mentioned this room having food and water, but all we managed to find were a couple boxes of water and a whole lot of baking supplies. By the end of our search, we had also found some metal mixing bowls, several small bags of powdered sugar, a few large bags of flour, and dozens of spatulas.

"Not even baker's chocolate." Victoria cursed and kicked a shelf, then made her way to the door. Just as she reached out to turn the knob, something slammed against the door hard enough to make it shake. We both froze as we waited to see if anything else would happen.

I could see her hand tremble as she continued to hold it outstretched while we waited. When the noise didn't repeat, Victoria took in a deep breath, let it out slowly, then put her hand on the doorknob.

"Do you really think it's smart to go out there right now?"

"I feel like my stomach is trying to eat itself. So it's either sit in here and starve to death, or go look for something to eat."

I looked at her, wondering if she was exaggerating. I wasn't even remotely hungry and she was claiming she was ravenous. It didn't make any sense. Although, losing two days worth of time didn't make much sense either.

"You can't go out there without anything to defend yourself." I grabbed two of the bags of sugar and ripped the tops off. She raised an eyebrow at me. I shrugged. "I dunno. Maybe it'll work as a distraction."

She nodded, and I moved to where I'd be able to toss the sugar in the face of whatever might be out there. It was pitiful, but I hoped it would buy us some time if we had to run. I raised one bag over my head and waited. After about thirty seconds it was still silent on the other side of the door, so I gave her a nod and she threw it open.

Nothing was out there, but there was a large patch of black sludge across the door. I slowly lowered the bag and licked my lips. I felt oddly calm as I peeked outside and looked up and down the hallway. Other than the smear, nothing looked out of the ordinary. There was absolutely no explanation for what had made the noise. Frowning, I stepped into the hall and Victoria followed.

"Come on. Let's go see if the others have any food to spare."

I led the way to the other door and used the same special knock Victoria had used before. I could hear movement behind the door, but nothing happened. I repeated the knock, as loud as I dared, looking up and down the hallway as I did. It was still empty, but if any of those things heard us, we'd be fucked.

Shuffling and what sounded like muffled voices came from behind the door and my mood went from annoyed to angry. First Darcie left me for dead, then the group thought I might be some sort of threat, and now they won't open the goddamn door? I'd had enough.

"It's us, you need to let us in! Now!"

Not bothering with the knock, I started banging on the door. My anxiety levels were beginning to rise; I knew I was making far more noise than I should. Victoria placed her hand on my shoulder, urging me to stop.

"Maybe Darcie convinced them to keep you out. We should go. This doesn't feel right."

Shrugging her off, I tried the knob and it turned easily in my hand. It was unlocked? Ignoring the small seed of dread that was blooming in my gut, I gripped the handle, twisted, and threw the door open.

I immediately understood why no one was coming to the door. The sludge had somehow gotten inside, and was *cov-*

ering the entryway. I ducked out of the way just as it shot out, slamming into the wall behind me. Victoria cried out, and now I could clearly hear the commotion coming from inside the room.

Looking up, I saw Shawn swinging a bat at a second pile of sludge, trying to keep it away from him, Darcie, and Irene. Alex and Sarah were on the other side of the room, cowering in a corner as a third piece of the sludge broke off from the rest and moved towards them.

"Dude! You gotta help us!" Shawn yelled as his bat sank into the black material. He pulled it back out, making a sickening sucking noise.

Before I could react, the sludge at the door had latched onto my leg. I didn't expect it to feel so...*warm*. It felt like it was crushing me and trying to devour me at the same time. It was the strangest, most terrifying sensation. Reacting purely on instinct, I threw sugar at it, getting it everywhere.

It recoiled immediately, and I could see the areas where the powder touched it starting to bubble and crack. Was it really that sensitive to the sugar? Instead of rearing up for a second attack, it slipped quickly down the hall and out of sight.

Back in the room, the slime creature had finished splitting into two. I only had one bag of sugar left. There was no way I'd have enough to stop both creatures. With no time to choose between the two groups, I took the bag and threw it.

I'd like to think I did it purely on instinct. That I had no bias whatsoever in my choice, and did it spur of the moment. However, I knew, deep down, that I didn't want to save Darcie. I let myself *hate* her. A glint of pure, unfiltered rage. The bag soared through the air and exploded against the creature descending on Alex and Sarah.

I heard a scream, and saw the other sludge monster diving towards Darcie, trying to envelop her. She darted out of the way, behind Irene, who wasn't able to dodge because of her chair. It was over in seconds. Irene didn't even get a chance to scream as whatever the hell these things were made out of began to dissolve her. Darcie grabbed Shawn's wrist and dragged him past me, pushing Victoria so hard that she fell on her ass.

I rushed over to Alex and Sarah, doing my best to avoid the convulsing black mass. It looked like it was in pain, but it wasn't making a sound, even though it was having the same reaction to the sugar as the slime in the hallway had. Enough of a reaction to slow it down, but hardly enough to stop it.

"Come on!" I grabbed Sarah's hand, assuming Alex would be right behind her. I glanced over at the thing consuming Irene, and hoped she hadn't suffered. I helped Victoria to her feet, and once the four of us were out of the room, I slammed the door shut. It felt like my heart was going to pound out of my chest. "How did they get in?!"

Alex shook his head. "I have no idea. We were all sleeping, and next thing I know There's a loud crash and Darcie is screaming her head off. The barricade in front of the door was gone and there was that sludge shit in the middle of the room. You burst in a few seconds later."

"We need to get out of here!" Victoria placed her hand on my shoulder, squeezing it tightly. I nodded my agreement without looking at her.

"We're too exposed. We need to regroup back in the other room to try to-"

"We need to get out of here NOW!" Victoria's hand jerked and forced me to turn. Two Shushers were running down the hall towards us. This was exactly what we didn't need.

'No! Fuck, no!" Sarah yelled, rather uncharacteristically, as she pushed past us and ran in the opposite direction. Not waiting a second longer, I followed quick on her heels. Alex and Victoria weren't far behind.

Bursting out of the double doors into the main food court area, I saw Darcie and Shawn turn a corner farther down the mall. Part of me wanted to run after her, make her pay for what she had done to myself and Irene, but there wasn't time for revenge with two skinless monsters right behind us.

"We're fucked. We're so fucked," Alex kept saying, over and over. He had a point: we had no weapons and no idea where to go. Looking around, I saw a high counter that was part of a Chinese buffet stall, and motioned for the others to follow me.

Jumping over the counter, I hid behind it as well as I could while the others joined me. Just as the last of us, Alex, began to crouch, I heard the double doors for the hallway slam open. Wet, meaty footsteps echoed across the food court as we did our best to remain silent.

The food above us smelled rotten, and it took every-thing in me not to gag. I thought these sorts of things were cleaned out every day, or had some sort of refrigeration, but I was just guessing. I had no idea how a mall food court worked. The mindlessness of it helped to calm my nerves, though, and I let my mind wander. My body, however, was ready to run if necessary.

The footsteps grew louder, until they stopped right in front of the buffet counter. I held my breath. When they just stood there, not moving, I knew we'd been caught. I wondered if we'd be able to get away, or if I had inadvertently picked the spot we'd all die in.

I shifted slightly, ready to jump back over the counter when something crashed in the distance. The Shushers took off at a run, their footsteps growing more and more distant until I couldn't hear them anymore.

We remained motionless for several more minutes, making sure the coast was clear. My legs were screaming from being crouched in an awkward position for so long and finally I had to stand. The food court, aside from a few bloody foot-prints, was empty.

"Thank god," Sarah said as she climbed over the counter. "They're gone."

"We need to find someplace safe, and figure out how the fuck to get out of here. I'm not going to fucking die in a mall." Alex sounded desperate and panicked. I agreed with him, but panic leads to mistakes, or selfish decisions like the ones Darcie had made.

If I saw her again, I swore I'd kill the bitch.

"Where the hell are we going? Nowhere is safe."

Sarah spoke in a soft whisper, wringing her hands. We had all taken to speaking far more quietly than normal, trying not to attract the attention of any more Shushers. I could only shrug in response. I was as clueless as she was.

"We need to fight back, find a way out of here." Victoria sounded determined, but looking at her face, I could see that she felt the same way I did: worn and broken.

"The sporting goods store, Hannigan's, and the food court are all compromised. What other options do we have?" I asked.

"You were outside, how bad was it? Really?"

I looked at Alex and tried to convey what I had seen as best I could.

"The whole area seems to be surrounded by some kind of black void. It starts a few feet into the parking lot and then there's just...nothing. Darkness, devoid of any light. The one security guard, Frank, actually went into it, back when this all started, but he was missing an arm when he came out. And...I think that black sludge is related to it somehow. You all heard what Darcie said about me and the stuff I threw up...and Emeline was outside as well."

As I explained things, Alex and Sarah backed away, putting distance between us. Even though I had saved their lives *twice*, he was still acting like I was some sort of threat. I balled my fists.

"Look, you want to go, then go. I may have puked up some of that shit, but I haven't exploded and I'm not dangerous. Sure, I was out there before anyone else was, but I also spent *less time* outside than anyone else had. If I was gonna go like a time bomb, don't you think I would've done it already?!"

My voice had gotten louder as I spoke, and Victoria made a motion for me to keep it down. I was done talking, anyway. I glared at Alex, who shrank under my gaze. At least Sarah seemed more appreciative now of what I had done for them.

"He's just scared. We all are. We can't stay out here in the open; we need to find someplace we can figure this out." She placed her hand on her husband's arm and I watched his shoulders slump. He closed his eyes and let out a deep sigh. This was getting to us. All of us.

"Alright. Let's get out of here and find some weapons. Maybe we can find a store that has a sturdy gate and no other way in or out. Someplace where we can hole up for a bit. So, before we leave the food court we should grab whatever food or water we can. Got it? *Five minutes.* I want us all back here in five minutes."

Everyone nodded at me and we split up. Truth be told, I just needed to get away from the rest of them for a few minutes, to let my head clear and organize my thoughts. Everything that had happened recently...it was just too much to process.

I walked over to one of the dessert cookie stalls, and peered around. Everything looked like it had been left out for weeks. Brownies and buns had thriving colonies of mold growing on them, while thinner, drier cookies had thick layers of dust. *Dust*? It made no sense. These things looked like they were *months* old.

Hopping over the counter, I looked inside the drink fridge. Most of the bottled juices had chunks floating in them, but the water looked okay. I thought about the sodas, but without knowing their condition inside the can, I decided they weren't worth the risk. There were only three, anyway.

The next two stalls I visited were the same: the food looked far older than it possibly could have been, even considering my missing two days. None of it made sense. What was causing the time gaps? Was it possible we had been here longer than we imagined?

When I figured that about five minutes had passed, I went back to the meeting point to take inventory of what I'd found. I had only managed to find four bottles of water, and a few candy bars. I ripped one open, just to see if it was edible. It looked fine, aside from the white residue that always formed on chocolate as it aged.

Victoria was the next one back. "Find anything useful?" she asked as she put three water bottles and three snack-sized bags of potato chips onto the table. I motioned to my haul, and she shook her head in disappointment. "I didn't do much better."

"Shit. We're gonna end up starving to death at this rate." I tossed her the open candy bar. "They look funny, but they're safe to eat. You said you were hungry earlier."

She caught it, but set it down, a sheepish look on her face. "Okay, admission time: I already ate the three bars that I found."

I should have been upset, given the situation we were in and how important it was to ration food, but I could only shake my head and smile. Besides, I highly doubted three candy bars were going to make the difference between life and death.

"We'll just say I gave you my share of the rations."

"Still not hungry?"

I hadn't realized until she said it, but I wasn't. There was food on the table, but I had only grabbed a candy bar. And I hadn't even opened it to eat, just to check if it was actually edible. "I guess not."

A minute later, Alex and Sarah made their way back. Neither had any food items, but they did have several bottles of water. At least we wouldn't go thirsty.

"Alright, looking at what we've got, we can each have four bottles of water. I think one a day will keep us going. We'll figure out how to divide the extra two bottles when the time comes. As for the food, we need to eat sparingly. No clue when we'll find more."

"So what now?" Victoria was looking right at me, and I took a moment to think about what to do next. The logical thing would be to try and figure out what had caused all this in the first place. I had to assume it was something either scientific or supernatural. But I wasn't great with science, and I sure as hell wasn't religious. I certainly wasn't the right person to lead these people to salvation.

"We try to not die. Come on."

I was leading our little group now, so when we left the food court I headed away from where the Shushers had pursued Darcie and Shawn. Not so much to avoid the creatures, but to avoid Darcie. Also, I wanted to pass the sporting goods store; we needed to try and find something to defend ourselves with.

"No! Get back!!"

We heard someone yelling in one of the stores ahead of us. I felt a strong urge to try and help, even though I was unarmed, but before I could take another step a figure stumbled out of the record store.

"David! Get out of there!"

I began to wonder who was ahead of us and why they would be trying to warn us, warn *me*, when the figure turned in our direction. Our eyes met and I froze, unable to move, breathe, or even think.

It was me. I was the one being attacked. A Shusher followed him out of the record store, heading straight towards him. I tried to say something, anything, but we were both in such shock that the other me barely reacted as the thing grabbed onto his head and tore it off with one clean jerk.

Two more people ran out of the store and headed in our direction. Frank, the security guard and the doctor. *The fucking security guard and the doctor were running towards us, both very much alive.*

"What the fuck is going on?!" Alex yelled as he watched them approach.

When Frank saw me, he did a double take, staring from the Shusher dragging my headless corpse back into the record store, then back to me. "The *fuck?!*"

"Worry about it later! There are more coming!!" the doctor yelled as he ran past us. "We have a safe spot in the food court!"

Instead of protesting, the four of us followed the two men, wondering what else could go wrong in the next few minutes. I felt light-headed, and everything was a blur. Back in the food court, they were about to open the door to the storage room when Alex stopped them.

"We can't go in there. That black shit is all over the place. We barely made it out alive the first time."

"First time? What are you talking about?" Frank pushed past Alex and yanked the door open. I couldn't bear to look, but I heard Sarah cry out in fear and surprise.

Victoria was standing next to Frank and let out a gasp. "Jesus Christ. This can't be possible."

Finally I turned to see. There wasn't a black sludge monster inside, waiting to devour us. Instead there was Irene, wheeling herself towards the door, looking at Alex, Sarah, and Victoria like they were ghosts.

"You...you're *dead*!!" I couldn't contain my surprise at seeing Irene.

"So are you." The doctor motioned towards me. "We just watched one of those skinless bastards rip the head off of *you*, yet it wasn't..."

We all stood there, looking at one another, dumbfounded, for what felt like hours. Frank finally realized how stupid it was to stand there gawking, and he broke the awkward silence that had descended.

"Let's get inside and sort this mess out. I'm getting a goddamn headache, and we're just fresh meat out here."

I eagerly followed the rest of them inside. I must have been staring at Irene without realizing it, because she shot me an odd look. "What the fuck is his problem? What the fuck happened out there? And why the fuck are *you* three standing here?!"

We couldn't help but look at one another sheepishly. We were as clueless as they were. Suddenly it wasn't so weird that I was missing two days. Was whatever happened to the mall causing some sort of time rift?

"Alternate dimensions." Alex said it softly at first, but then he started to nod furiously to himself. "It's gotta be some sort of...pocket dimension that folds all others in on themselves!"

No one else had a better answer, and I guess it made a modicum of sense when you got right down to it. It explained why people who had died right in front of us were standing here alive again.

"Okay," I said slowly, as I let the ideas work themselves through in my head, "let's say that *is* true. It still doesn't explain how or why this is happening. It also doesn't explain why there are skinless monsters and piles of black slime hunting us."

Alex shrugged, looking defeated. "I dunno. I just saw something like this on TV once."

"No, no. I think Alex has a point. We still have no idea how this began, but if we can figure out what's happening, maybe we can reverse it." Frank seemed almost hopeful about the whole predicament.

I was still trying to process having watched my own violent death. The fact that I had seen my spinal column. The inside of my neck and throat. My lifeless eyes frozen open in terror...I still felt light headed.

"Guys, I don't...I don't think...I..."

I couldn't get the words out. I couldn't think straight. My whole body went limp and my vision became blurry. I barely registered Victoria speaking to me as I blacked out, falling to the floor.

XI

I was in another nightmare, only this time I *knew* I was in one. I'd never been a lucid dreamer, but this time, for some reason, I was fully cognizant of my actions and surroundings. It was vividly real, and they only thing that gave away the fact it was a dream was that I was *watching* myself, from above.

I was in the middle of a field of corn, the stalks taller than I was, except the colors were all wrong. The stalks were a sickly grey color, as if all the life had been sucked out of them, and they would crumble like ash as I brushed past them, leaving a residue on my skin and clothes. The sky was dark crimson, and cloudless.

I could feel it calling to me, that same dark presence from before, only this time I didn't think of it as a god. I just knew it was something larger and more powerful than I could ever be, and it wanted me to become...part of it? Worship it? No...*serve* it. As that became clearer, it was more and more incessant.

Every fiber of my being rejected its advances, and I could feel anger welling up around me. I tried to run but found I was starting to sink into the ground. I clawed at the cornstalks around me, trying to stop myself from sinking, but they were suddenly *gone*. There was no escape. I was destined to live and die at the whim of this malevolent creature.

I was buried waist deep now, and I called out to whatever was causing this. Called for it to stop what it was doing and let me live. I began to beg for my life. Pleading, crying, and blubbering as I sank lower and lower, I was revolted by the depths I was apparently willing to sink to in my desperate bid for self preservation.

The one thing I did not do, however, was agree to serve it. I could feel its frustration. I felt stabbing pains up and down my legs as something under the muck attacked me, ripping at my flesh, but I still would not relent and worship it.

I was up to my neck now. Snot and tears streamed down my face, but I still did not agree to *its* terms. As much as I wanted to live, I knew giving into it would destroy my soul. Slowly my face started to submerge, and I refused to accept my fate. I took in a breath, as deep as I could manage, and shut my eyes tight. If I was going to die, it wasn't going to be easily. Whatever was doing this would have to work to take me.

As soon as my head went under, I was no longer watching. I was now experiencing it all first hand. I expected to begin drowning in mud and muck. Instead I was falling through a black space, twisting and twirling in the air as I tried to get some sort of bearing on where I was headed.

There, waiting below me, was a massive spider. Even in the pure black abyss, it was as easy to see as if it were lit by the noonday sun. It looked like a hellish cross between a tarantula and a black widow. Massive fangs opened, oozing putrid venom and waiting for its snack, me, to fall into its jaws.

I screamed.

*****

The dream didn't end there, but thankfully I could remember little else when I awoke. I felt like I had been asleep for hours, but apparently I had only been unconscious for fifteen or twenty minutes. Alex, Sarah and Victoria were arguing with Frank and the doctor, while Irene was watching over me.

"Guys, he's awake."

Everyone turned their attention to me as I groggily sat up. Big mistake. My head was throbbing and I let out a hiss as I put my palm to my forehead.

"Easy. We tried to catch you, but your fainting caught us off guard. You banged your head pretty good on the shelf. No blood, but I have no idea if you have a concussion or not," Irene explained. I gently nodded my understanding, and tried not to move too much.

"What's going on? Why is everyone arguing?" I asked.

Alex and Frank both began to speak at once, but Alex backed down after Frank glared at him. "We're trying to figure out what the hell is going on. According to you three," he motioned at Alex, Sarah and Victoria, "Randall, Irene, and I are dead. According to *us*, we've never met any of you, and Randall and I just watched David die. Well, *a* David."

It sounded insane when said aloud. What was even more strange was that they recognized me but not the others. "You really have no idea who they are?"

"Nope, never seen them in my life."

"Look, why don't you bring us up to speed? Maybe we can figure out how we fit together." Sarah mentioned.

"We've been *trying* you dumb bitch. But *he*," Frank pointed at Alex, "won't shut his yap for five seconds."

"That was uncalled for, Frank." Irene glared at him, and I could see his rough demeanor soften. Avoiding eye contact with Sarah, he apologized. She said nothing.

"About four hours ago-"

"That's impossible." Alex interrupted.

"We aren't going to get anywhere if you don't let them speak," Victoria said. I agreed with her. Alex seemed to sense this was a losing battle and folded his arms indignantly.

"As I was saying, around four hours ago all contact with anything or anyone outside the mall ceased. A dark barrier surrounded us on all sides, and anyone who dies tends to come back as a skinless abomination. We were out getting supplies when we encountered one of them and ran into your group. That's when *our* David was killed."

I stood on wobbly legs, ignoring the pain from the side of my head. "You said this all started four hours ago and yet you've managed to find shelter, do minor fortifications, and even go on scouting missions to gather supplies? Alex can be insufferable at times, but he has a point. That's impossible."

"Not really. I do apocalypse training and drills as a hobby. Keeps my mind sharp." Frank beamed. "I saw this as an opportunity."

"Without Frank, who knows how things might have turned out," Irene added.

I had a pretty solid idea. "Are there more of you? What about your son?" I asked the doctor.

He looked surprised I had even mentioned his son. "No, we were the only ones, aside from David...the *other* David. Anyone else we encountered had either already been turned into one of the skinless or was in the midst of being killed by them. My son, thank god, is home with his wife and family."

"Good. We watched him die and then kill you."

The color drained from Randall's face, and he leaned back against the wall. He slowly licked his lips and took in a ragged breath, but his face was devoid of emotion. It struck me as odd, but I ignored it and continued. "Frank, do you have a partner named Daniel?"

Frank nodded. "Yeah, he was killed at the start. He and I went outside to investigate and something pulled him into that black void surrounding the mall. He never came back out."

Had that happened to our version of Daniel? Was his Daniel the one that attacked us? My head was starting to hurt more as I tried to wrap my head around different versions of each of us, all experiencing the same hell. How many were there? Was there yet *another* me out there, being killed, as we all sat in safety and chatted like a sewing circle?

"Whatever the fuck is going on, we need to find a way to get out of here." Victoria's voice brought me out of the swirling confusion in my mind.

"I concur," Randall agreed, his face looking more flush with color. "If we stay here too long, we'll die."

Alex had been quiet after we shushed him, but he suddenly had a look of panic in his eyes. "Frank, did you say you went outside?!"

He nodded. "Yeah, Daniel and I went to chec-"

"We need to get out of here, now!" Alex yelled as he grabbed Sarah's hand. It took me a moment to realize what he was worried about: Frank exploding from the black sludge. Truth be told, we only *assumed* it was caused by going outside. I had been outside but the worst I did was throw up. What if it was simply this place?

"You're being irrational. Just because it happened once doesn't mean it will happen again." I tried to calm him down, but he was having none of it. He barged towards the door and threw it open, heading into the hallway.

"Fucking knock it off! If you make too much noise you'll attract them!" Frank spit out in a harsh whisper. The couple was already well down the hall and almost to the exit that led back to the food court.

I looked at Victoria. "We have to get them back. If only for Sarah's sake." She nodded in agreement and we both headed after them. They had already made their way out of the hallway, and Victoria was about to follow but she glanced out the small window on the door and stopped. Tears welled up in her eyes and she brought her hand to her mouth.

Fearing the worst, I looked out as well. Alex and Sarah were surrounded by several of the Shushers. Alex was cowering in the center of the group while Sarah wailed, but the Shushers weren't doing anything about the noise. They were just standing there, like perimeter guards of some kind. I wanted to rush out and help, knock a few of those things aside so they could get to safety, but what I saw next chilled me to my soul.

A man, or something in the shape of a man, entered the food court. It was at least six feet tall, maybe more, and had the body of an Adonis It was also stark naked, save for a rough loincloth barely covering his groin. It's skin was a sickly shade of green, and looked dried out and cracked. It's head was the skull of a bull, with two blood red horns jutting asymmetrically from the sides. I didn't know what else to call it, so I christened it the Minotaur.

The Shushers parted so it could enter the circle, and Sarah lost her mind. She bolted for the opening, and, surprisingly, the thing let her pass. It must have been too focused on Alex. He just stood there, trembling. I couldn't hear what he said, but I could tell he was begging for his life.

The Minotaur stood before Alex for at least a minute, listening to him beg and plead, before it reached out and grabbed his arm, near the elbow, and lifted him into the air. I could hear his screams now as he struggled against his attacker, kicking and flailing as he tried to get away. The Minotaur then grabbed his shoulder firmly with one hand and yanked hard on the arm with the other.

Blood gushed from Alex's arm as he screamed and cried. The Minotaur dropped him and I saw only bones where

Alex's arm should have been. In a single motion, the creature had somehow stripped the arm of all flesh.

I could see that Alex was losing it, going into shock; he barely registered when the Minotaur did the same thing to his other arm, then tore apart his legs. Then it gathered up all the...meat it had acquired and left. The Shushers turned and left as well, and, as soon as we were certain that they were long gone, we quietly made our way out of the hallway and moved towards Alex.

He was dead. In fact, I was pretty sure he had been dead since the Minotaur peeled the flesh from his other arm. Seeing his body there, on the ground, was surreal. He had been alive not five minutes ago, and now he was a torso with bones sticking out of it, like some kind of gory children's toy.

Victoria and I were about to leave when Alex's eyes shot open. He looked right at me, smiled, and then started to scream.

"SERVE ME DAVID! CUT THE BITCH! SERVE ME! SERVE ME! SERVE! SERVE! SERVE! SERVE YOU FUCKING BASTARD!!

Something in me snapped, and I stomped on his smug, asshole face. I didn't stop stomping until my shoe was slick with blood and gore, and his head wasn't even recognizable as human. Why had he said those things? How had he known about my dreams?!

"We need to get back to the others before that thing comes back."

I looked at Victoria. Was she the 'bitch' I was supposed to cut? "I'm fucking sick of this place." I pushed past her and led the way back.

XII

Shushers. Black goo. A fucking *Minotaur*. Whatever the hell was going on, it seemed to be getting worse. I thought about trying to track down Sarah, but she had been so panicked when she ran off that I didn't think she would be coherent enough to understand we were trying to help her. I looked to Victoria, and she quickly avoided my gaze. Had what Alex said gotten to her? What I had done to his head?

"Look, what he said..."

"Doesn't matter, does it? He could've been talking about me or about his wife. Or about someone else. But do you know *why* it doesn't matter?" She looked right at me, tears in her eyes. "We're all going to fucking die here. We're already dead."

She quickened her pace to walk ahead of me and I didn't know what to say. What *could* I say to respond to something like that? Especially since we both knew it was true.

We got back to the hideout without speaking another word to each other. When the others saw us, their shoulders slumped and their faces became drawn; they knew we'd lost Alex and Sarah.

"So what's the plan?" I looked to Frank, hoping he had something, anything, we could latch onto. Some sliver of hope.

"While you guys were gone, I had an epiphany."

"Oh?" Randall seemed genuinely surprised. Frank must not have shared this idea yet.

"Yeah," Frank continued, "it's stupidly simple, honestly."

"Spit it out," Irene commanded.

"There's a panic room near the center of the mall, on the basement level. It's got enough food and supplies to last for weeks. We could just wait this whole thing out down there."

"Why the *fuck* did you not tell us sooner?!" Irene was the one to voice her concerns, but both she and Randall looked pissed. Frankly, so was I.

The Frank I met first had died before he had a chance to share any useful information, but I couldn't understand why *this* Frank hadn't told anyone this before. In the midst of this hell, why had he neglected to mention a possible safe haven until after so many people had been killed?!

"I figured it was too much of a long shot. Besides, I..."

"What?" Victoria asked.

"Well...see, I know the code to get in, but I don't know EXACTLY where it is. Just that it's somewhere near the center of the lower level. I don't even know if the entrance is hidden or not."

"Do you care to explain how you know the code to this top secret room? The one that you don't even know the location of?" The doctor did little to hide the doubt that was thick in his voice. And honestly, I agreed with him. This seemed too convenient, too easy. Part of me screamed that we should ignore whatever Frank said next, but the hope of survival was too much to suppress.

"My brother-in-law worked construction for the lower levels. They swore his entire crew to secrecy and made them all sign iron-clad non-disclosure agreements. Then, after they sealed it all up, they brought in a different crew to finish the mall. "

"And why did he tell *you*?" More doubt from the doctor.

"How the fuck should I know? That asshole was drunk off his ass. I never paid much attention to it, but he said a whole bunch of really weird shit and he gave me the code."

"Like what?" Doubt or not, he had me intrigued.

"He told me that if I took the job here, I'd regret it. If I lived long enough. Made no fucking sense to me until we saw those skinless shits."

Secret levels, hidden panic rooms...this was heading way too far into conspiracy theory territory, and it was starting to make Alex's theory sound downright believable. I shook my head to clear it, and looked right at Frank.

"How do we get to the lower level? Even the department stores aren't part of that network. Hell, I didn't even know malls *had* a basement level."

"Most don't. There aren't even any security cameras down there or anything. But I'm telling you, that's where we need to go if we want to survive this thing. I shoulda brought it up sooner," he looked right at the doctor, "but like I said, I wasn't sure."

The rest of us looked at each other. We were downtrodden, beaten, and tired. The thought of finding a safe place, a *truly* safe place...it was more than enough for all of us to feel a little better. This was the hope we needed.

"Alright. You need to get us to the basement. If we haven't found the panic room after being down there for an hour, we come back here. Assuming we're still alive. Agreed?" The doctor looked at each of us in turn, and we all nodded.

He'd talked about us still being alive in an hour as if it was no more than a possibility, but he was right. This panic room idea was not guaranteed. Just some second-hand drunken ramblings. I glanced over at Victoria and we shared a look; a silent agreement not to mention the Minotaur. No sense adding more panic to the situation. Besides, if it showed up again, there would be plenty of panic to go around.

Leaving the room was surreal. We took all of the supplies with us, firmly believing that we wouldn't be coming back. Either because the panic room existed, or that there wouldn't *be* anyone to come back. I was the last one out, and I felt compelled to turn off the light as I shut the door. It felt like we were walking from one tomb to another.

According to Frank the service elevator to the basement was right next to the security offices. Thankfully we didn't encounter anything on our way back to the mall's main concourse. As we neared our destination, I was so focused on looking for movement around us, that the sound of Victoria's sudden gasping caused my heart to pound in my chest. I spun on my feet, ready to run, when my jaw dropped.

We were walking past one of the entrances to the mall, but outside was...different now. Instead of an endless black void that went on forever, the sky was a crimson canvas. Instead of a parking lot, there was a forest outside. It started a few dozen feet away from the doors and grew more and more dense the further back it went. I could not see through to the other side.

It was a breathtaking view, but it caused the blood to freeze in my veins. It reminded me far too much of my dreams. Far too much of that dark, sinister presence trying to corrupt me. I turned away from it, and was surprised to find that my brow was covered in sweat and I was breathing heavily. The others seemed unaffected by it, aside from being shocked by its sudden appearance.

"We need to get to that panic room. Wait this out." I tried to get the group moving again.

"Do we? That void is gone! We might be able to get out of here! We have to at least try!"

Did we? Randall's words were impassioned, but did little to convince me. I only sensed death and terror beyond those doors. At least in the panic room there was a chance to wait this out. It was cowardly, sure, but the feeling I got from this new area was...unsettling.

"No, David is right," Frank agreed with me. "We have no idea if that's even fucking *real* out there. Could be some sort of trap."

"But what if it's the way out?! We can't just ignore this!" Irene made her choice and wheeled over to the doctor.

That just left Victoria. I looked over at her, about to plead my case to try and get her to join us when Randall spoke.

"We're at a stalemate, it seems. I don't want to be a sitting duck out here, and I think Irene can agree that we should stay together as a team, not split up. Since it's two and two, that makes you, Victoria, the tie breaker. Can everyone agree that we'll follow her vote?"

Putting my life into her hands like that made me even more uneasy than the forest did. Even though I trusted her now, I didn't like the idea of someone else's decision determining if I lived or died. If such a choice was to be made, I wanted it to be my own.

"Agreed." Frank apparently spoke for the rest of us. I frowned at him, but made no further protest.

"Alright, then. Victoria, what will we do?"

She took a moment to stare out at the forest, gazing past the trees. I couldn't be certain, but it looked like she was trying to focus on something out there. I tried to look in the same general direction that she was, but I couldn't see anything remarkable, other than a few trees that were an odd, ashen hue.

Shaking her head, she turned back to the rest of us. "We should..." Her eyes grew wide, and her jaw dropped as she cut herself off. I turned to see what had gotten her attention, a knot forming in the pit of my stomach.

I expected Shushers or black goo. Instead it was the Minotaur. It was just coming around a corner, and it was *eating* something. As it drew closer I saw that it was skin and muscle; most likely Alex's. What was even more disturbing was that Sarah was right behind him; stark naked, covered in blood, but very much alive.

Her hair was slick, sticking to her face in matted lumps, and her eyes were wild. Her mouth was open in a fiendish grin, and as soon as she saw us, she pointed and yelled, "FEAST! FEAST!!"

Whatever had happened to her, I didn't want to stick around to find out. The Minotaur had made our choice for us. Victoria was already on her way out the doors, and I was hot on her heels.

As we stepped outside, the air made me cough. It was breathable, and thankfully cool, but there was an unmistakable smell of decay. Not the decay of flesh, but of old growth...vegetation left to rot. It was an underlying, cloying scent, but it was present enough that it was hard to ignore. The closer we got to the forest, the stronger it smelled.

"Something isn't right. We shouldn't go in there," I tried to protest.

"You want to find out what *that* fucking thing wants?" Frank retorted.

"Was that Sarah? What happened to her?!" Victoria called over her shoulder as she darted in between the trees.

The three of us were making out way easily through the dense foliage, zigging and zagging around the trunks.

"Fuck! Don't leave me!!"

I turned back and realized there was no way Irene could make it through a landscape like this in her chair. She was still at the edge of the forest.

"Fuck, we gotta go back!" Frank yelled out, turning back to help her. I turned around as well; we didn't have much time, and I didn't know if he would be strong enough to carry her.

The Minotaur literally *burst* out of the mall, glass and metal from the doors flying everywhere. In spite of the shrapnel, though, the beast appeared unharmed. It charged towards Irene, while Frank and I ran as fast as we could, trying to get to her first.

"I don't want to fucking die!" Irene yelled, trying to get her chair between two narrowly spaced trees.

"Forget the chair!" I grabbed her arm and pulled her out of the chair just as a fist came crashing down where she had been sitting. The wheelchair crumpled immediately, as if it were made of paper. The beast cried out in anger, and swung its arms wildly. Frank tried to avoid the blow, but it clipped him, and sent him flying out of the forest. Sarah, who had been running to catch up, pounced on him.

"Get her off of me!!" He yelled, struggling with her. The fact that she was covered in blood made it more difficult, and his hands just slid across her skin as he tried to grab her and push her away.

"FEAST 'N FUCK! FEAST 'N FUCK!!"

She started humping him, and he finally got the leverage to push her away. She landed on her ass, crying out in pain. The sound caught the attention of the Minotaur, and it stomped towards them.

"RUN!" I screamed, hoping Frank could get back to the treeline before the Minotaur caught him.

He scrambled to his feet, and managed to dodge as the Minotaur grabbed at him. I hoisted Irene onto my back as he made his way back to me, stumbling.

"GO!"

We ran as fast as we could, but I could feel my legs begin to burn from the extra weight. As much as I hated to admit it, I wasn't willing to die for Irene. If I had to drop her to save myself, I would.

"Hold up. Stop!" Randall called to us. He and Victoria were still standing about where they'd been when we went back to try and help Irene. I slowed down and dared a glance behind me.

Both the Minotaur and Sarah were standing at the edge of the forest, glaring at us. While the thing was massive, it could have easily made its way through the trees. Something was *keeping* them out of the forest. Or they had the good sense not to come inside. I tried not to think about what could make monsters afraid.

As we stood there, staring at each other, I saw Sarah reach under the thing's loin cloth with one hand. A moment later her other hand ripped away the flimsy garment, exposing his shaft as she stroked it. Then she climbed him, impaling herself on his jutting member. When the motion of her hips became a determined frenzy and she started squealing in orgasmic pleasure, I finally turned away.

This place was a fucking wonderland.

XIII

Since we were in no immediate danger, and weren't being followed, we decided to conserve our strength as we made our way through the forest. The going was rough, but not because of the trees. Oddly enough, the trees seemed to be spaced pretty evenly. It was the undergrowth that was causing trouble; it was getting more and more dense the deeper we went into the woods. We had no means of cutting it back, so we were forced to push our way through.

"We're going to die out here."

Frank's voice surprised me, but only because no one had said anything since we left Sarah and the Minotaur behind. I wanted to disagree with him, but everything that was happening seemed to have driven us to this place. A foreign landscape, little food or water, and no idea where we were going or what we would do if we actually managed to get somewhere.

"Maybe. Most certainly if you have that attitude. We aren't dead yet, though, are we?" Randall moved past Frank as he spoke, heading to the front of the group. From where I was, I saw Frank's body tense, then relax a few seconds later. Apparently he didn't like the good doctor taking the lead like that.

"What-the-fuck-ever, *Doc*. Say we *are* finally safe from whatever shit got into the mall. We're gonna starve out here. Or worse. Unless you got another miracle plan to save us."

Another? What had Frank meant? I didn't like his tone, either. I was going to say something, but apparently Irene *also* didn't like his tone; I could feel her nails dig deeply into my shoulder, and the pain distracted me.

"Ow," I muttered under my breath.

Realizing what she was doing, she eased her grip. "Shit. Sorry, David."

"It's alright. We're all on edge."

I looked over at Victoria. She was keeping pace with me as the other two took point, still arguing about the futility of our excursion. Her face was blank, but her gait was determined.

"What do you think?" I asked her.

It took her a minute to realize I was talking to her, and it seemed to break her out of some kind of trance. She blinked several times before answering. "Think about what?"

I motioned to Randall and Frank. They'd both shut up by this time. "Those two. They were arguing about whether or not we're going to die out here. Randall has a more optimistic view than Frank."

She shrugged. "We're going to die out here, I guess. Unless a miracle happens." She looked up at the bits of red sky that filtered through the treetops, shaking her head. "This doesn't feel like a place that a miracle could happen. Does it?"

"This place feels like the grave," Irene spoke up, answering for me. I didn't correct her.

Frank hurried towards us, motioning for us to quiet down. "Shh! We think we found something! Over here."

Curious about what they may have found, we stopped talking and made our way over to where Randall was waiting. We had been walking in a relatively straight line since we entered the forest, but he had veered off our 'path' by about twenty feet. Considering how dense the underbrush was, I wondered how he managed to spot anything.

We pulled a few ashen leaves out of the way so we could all see. There was a clearing in the forest, about fifteen feet in diameter. In the center of the clearing was a strange structure. It was eight or nine feet tall, and seemed to be a solid cube, made of some dark green material. I started to move forward, into the clearing, when Randall put his hand on my chest and shook his head, pointing at something.

Following his finger, I watched and waited. For thirty or forty seconds nothing happened, but then a mouse came out from around the other side of the cube. It looked *normal*. I don't know why I was expecting some sort of hellish version of a mouse, but I was surprised that there was nothing obviously wrong with it. What the hell did it mean?

Another few seconds and another mouse came around the other side. We all watched in stunned silence as they explored around the cube; sniffing the air, eyes darting around, forever on the lookout for predators.

"Where the fuck did they come from?" Irene asked, too loudly. One of the animals stood on its hind legs, nose twitching, and looked in our direction. A moment later both mice were gone, having run back around the cube.

"Well, fuck it. Nature walk is over. What is this thing?"

Frank pushed past me and out into the open, walking towards the structure. He circled around to where the mice had disappeared, and I was expecting him to come back around the other side.

When he didn't immediately come back into view Randall called out to him. "Frank?". There was no reply, and a bolt of panic and fear hit me in the gut. Was this thing what the Minotaur was afraid of?

'Frank!" Calling louder, Randall stepped into the clearing. I wanted to follow, but something in the back of my head was screaming at me to get out of there, to get as far away as possible. Instead of listening, I just stood there, frozen.

"What? You guys gotta see this!" Frank's voice came from behind the cube. I let out a sigh of relief, not even realizing I had been holding my breath. I held the brush out of the way for Victoria, then entered the clearing myself. I felt Irene struggle a bit.

"Fuck, David! Thanks for keeping it out of *my* face."

"Sorry." I looked around the clearing, and the feeling of panic and dread from a moment ago felt even more heightened. But there was an odd feeling of calm with it now. Almost peace. It was as if I *knew* that death was just seconds away, but my mind had not only gotten used to the idea, it welcomed it. I didn't want to stay in the clearing any longer than we had to.

We made our way around to where Frank was standing and I gasped. There was an opening in the cube, like a door, but what shocked me was what appeared to be *inside* the cube.

Inside...seemed to be the mall. Well, *part* of the mall, at least. It looked like some sort of jewelry store.

"Is this...some sort of portal?" Irene asked no one in particular.

"I have no idea, but that makes as much sense as anything else." As soon as Randall finished speaking, we watched the two mice scurry across the floor towards a small hole in the wall, near a display case.

"Alternate dimensions, portals in the middle of forests...what the fuck is this place?"

"I don't know, David. But considering what we've seen, it stands to reason that the mall has somehow been transported to another plane of existence. Another dimension. And in the process, rifts like this have been torn open." Randall tried his best to explain, but saying it out loud like that just made everything sound even more insane than it already felt.

"Do we go through it?" Victoria was standing just behind me.

"Do you think it's safe?" Irene asked.

Randall was standing in front of the doorway. Portal? I didn't know what to call it. I didn't know what to make of any of this. Just trying to think about this place in logical terms was starting to make my head hurt. I wanted to go home. I should have just given my nephew cash.

"I don't know if it's safe or not, but it can get us back into the mall, and then we can try to head for the panic room Frank was telling us about. It's our best bet. We *need* to get to that room." Randall stared straight ahead while he spoke. He was suddenly adamant about getting to that room, and it bothered me.

Up to this point he had seemed as confused and terrified as the rest of us. Hell, I had watched him and his son *die*. But now? Now he was calm, collected. As if he had a new purpose.

"That's a good idea. If that cow-fuck and Sarah are still at the edge of the forest, we can avoid them and run straight for the room. I say we go for it."

Frank took a step forward, and stuck his arm out. The act struck me as odd, and I couldn't place why. There was just an unmistakable sensation that all this was wrong. Not just the strange portal doorway thing in a green cube in an alien forest, everything.

He continued to move forward, hesitating just before his hand crossed the threshold. He took in a breath to steel himself, then shoved his arm through. He stumbled a bit, probably because he had been expecting resistance and there was none. Then he just stood there with his arm through the doorway.

"Huh. It doesn't feel any different at-"

A bloody, skinless hand grabbed Frank's arm, wrenching it to an unnatural angle. I heard something snap, and Frank began to scream. I quickly dropped Irene as Randall and I grabbed onto him, to try and pull him back, but I felt far too weak from carrying her, and Randall couldn't seem to get much of a grip.

The Shusher came into view, one hand still holding Frank's wrist. It used the other hand to grip his forearm, and with one twist, finished breaking it. Then, with one hard tug, Frank's hand and forearm were gone. Frank fell back and I realized why everything had felt so off to me.

The arm Frank had put through the portal was the same one that the other Frank had lost. The wound was *identical*. Somehow, this was *that* Frank, but such a thing was impossible.

Blood splashed against the cube, and was immediately absorbed. Randall took a step back and watched with what I could only describe as utter fascination. The cube began to change color, becoming a dark purple, and the portal to the mall melted away into a black nothingness. The same black void that had surrounded the mall when all this began.

Victoria grabbed my arm and swung me around. "We have to get the hell out of here!"

"What about Frank?!" I yelled, turning back.

Frank was laying on the ground about ten feet away, writhing in agony, and clutching his ruined stump of an arm. He tried to get up, looking to Randall for help. I watched in shock as Randall moved towards him, helped him up, and then smirked.

"This has happened before, hasn't it? It's all a goddamn paradox now, isn't it?" He laughed and shook his head. Frank looked pained and confused.

"W-what the h-hell are you t-talking about?" Frank managed to get out, his breathing ragged.

"I'm talking about time. I'm talking about control. Time to face destiny, Frank." With that, Randall pushed Frank through the empty doorway. He turned to look back at me, winked, and then walked through after him. Once both men had gone through, the doorway disappeared. After a moment the cube began to sink into the ground. It continued to burrow deeper into the dirt, leaving a hole behind it. Still feeling the ground rumble, I dared to creep forward and look down into the pit it had created.

It was beginning to fill with the same black sludge from before. Only there was so much of it that it seemed impossible. I could see it trying to climb up the walls, impatient to leave its prison.

It would be upon us in a matter of seconds.

XIV

"We need to get the fuck out of here!" Irene yelled into my ear as I picked her back up, temporarily deafening me. I winced slightly but kept staring at the sludge as it got closer and closer to the top of the pit. Something felt...off about how it was moving.

It wasn't moving the way the creature had before; it wasn't oozing, just bubbling as it filled the pit. I realized that it might *not* be one of the creatures, and stood my ground. A few seconds later my gambit paid off: as it came even with the surface, the ooze solidified and turned to dirt. It was as if the cube had never been there.

I could feel Irene's whole body slump as her head hit my shoulder and she let out a sob. "What the fuck *is* this place? I just want to go home."

We were in no immediate danger, so I helped her off of my back again, and the three of us sat there, next to the square patch on the ground, taking a moment to rest.

"Sarah has gone batshit, Frank is probably dead, and Randall..." Victoria let her voice trail off.

"He has to be connected to all of this, I'm just not sure how." I finished her sentence.

The other two didn't acknowledge my words, but I had a feeling they agreed with me. Or, they just didn't want to argue about it. Neither did I. We were all haggard, had no food or water, and were stuck in some god-forsaken forest.

I felt like we had been backed into a corner, and I had no clue how to proceed. How on earth *could* we proceed? The only hope for safety was getting to that panic room, but Frank was the only person who had the code. Not to mention, we didn't know what horrors we'd have to face while trying to find it. I turned to look deeper into the forest. The trees grew more and more dense, and I could only see for a few dozen yards before they completely blocked my vision.

"We need to go back." Victoria stood and brushed herself off as she spoke. She looked at me and Irene, before continuing. "If we stay out here, we'll die."

"How can you be so sure? Here is the only place where nothing has tried to fucking kill us." Irene spat out defiantly.

"Only because nothing was willing to follow us in here! That Minotaur bastard just stood there at the edge, like it *knew* something." Victoria looked upward, frowning. "I don't know what passes for day or night around here, but it's been getting darker. Do you want to stay here and find out what happens when *all* the light goes out?"

A sudden chill went up my spine, and I had to agree with her. At least we could run and hide from the things inside the mall. Out here, there was nowhere to hide, and running could only get you so far.

"Alright. Let's go back."

"No. No fucking way!"

I turned to Irene, wondering how I could convince her. The most obvious solution was also the most blunt. "If you don't come, we'll leave you here. How far do you think you'll get without the use of your legs?"

"Fuck you, you *bastard.*"

She seethed at me, but made no effort to push me or Victoria away as we lifted her onto my back again. I could already feel my muscles straining. I wished that there had been some way to save her chair.

"So once we get back, what's the plan?" I asked Victoria.

She looked into the distance for a moment, before heading back the way we came.

"Try not to die."

*****

The walk back to the mall seemed to take three times as long as the walk into the woods had. Maybe because now we weren't running for our lives, or maybe because this time we walked in silence. After Victoria's statement, none of us had anything else to say. I thought about speaking several times, but anything I said would have been heavy and forced.

The trees thinned the closer we got to the mall. In fact, there were drastically fewer trees now than there had been when we ran into the forest. Thinking about it was causing a dull ache at the base of my brain though, so I tried not to focus on it. *Nothing makes sense here*, I kept repeating to myself. *Nothing makes sense.* The mantra helped to calm me. Somewhat.

The crimson sky was nearly jet black now, and the only illumination was coming from the mall itself. I swore I heard something slithering behind us, but we were so close to our goal that I didn't want to cause anyone panic by mentioning it. Mostly, I didn't want to cause *myself* to panic.

Victoria, who was just ahead of me, stopped suddenly and took a step back. I almost ran into her, and was about to ask her what was going on when she grabbed my arm and squeezed, pointing with her free hand. I followed her finger until I saw a prone figure lying near the doorway to the mall. But this doorway showed no damage from the Minotaur bursting through. Had we gotten turned around in the woods, and wound up at another entrance?.

It took only a second to realize that the figure was Sarah. Remembering the slithering noise, I looked behind us and peered into the forest. Was the Minotaur sneaking up behind us in some sort of ambush? If he *was* out there, he was biding his sweet time.

"We need to get past Sarah without alerting her," I whispered to Victoria.

Irene stirred on my back, and I turned my head to try and see her. Her lips were nearly touching my ear, and she spoke as quietly as I had

"We need to kill her. It's the only way."

"Are you crazy?? We can't just kill Sarah," I protested.

"She was willing to kill us. She *fucked* that thing while we ran for our lives. She doesn't deserve to live."

Victoria didn't interject as Irene and I argued about Sarah's fate, but she raised a finger to her lips when Irene's voice began to get louder. We both shut up, but she looked so much like one of the Shushers in the dim light...it made me uneasy.

"We compromise. If we're quiet, maybe we can sneak past. If she wakes up, we kill her," Victoria stated coldly. I nodded, and felt Irene nod reluctantly behind me.

We started off slowly, but once we were past the treeline I felt very exposed. We picked up the pace, making sure to step softly as we got closer to where Sarah was lying on the ground. It was impossible to keep our distance; she was almost right in front of the door.

Victoria had pulled ahead of me, and I was still a few feet away when she managed to ease the door open. I was next to Sarah, thinking I'd managed to sneak past, when she rolled over. She was wide awake and smiling, her teeth caked with blood and gore.

"You here for the feast?" she asked, licking her lips. Then she ran her hands over her body, cupping her breasts. "Or are you here to *fuck?*"

I was stammering like an idiot, trying to answer her, when Victoria yelled at me. "Get in here! Now!"

I looked up and saw that she was looking past me, not at me. I turned around, and saw something that defied all logic, even in this hellish place.

The trees were *bent*. No other word could accurately describe it; they were at odd, unnatural angles, but not broken or splintered. They had opened to form a path through the forest, making way for something that was crawling towards us. Fast. It was a mass of tentacles, with dozens of grotesque eyes along the length of each one. It writhed and squirmed out from behind the trees, pulling itself forward on two giant tentacles, each at least five feet thick.

In the middle of this mass, was a giant eye with a sharp, serrated beak jutting right out of the center of the iris. The creature stopped moving when it saw us, and everything was silent for a moment. Then it opened its mouth and let out a sound that I felt more than heard. As it washed over me it felt like my mind was under assault, fighting to maintain sanity. I screamed in terror. Irene let go of my shoulders and fell to the ground, clutching her head.

I couldn't see Victoria, but Sarah seemed unfazed by whatever this thing was. In fact, she seemed downright *delighted* to see it.

Serve me.

The voice from my dreams rushed into my head, causing me to drop to my knees. I looked and realized that this had to be the dark 'god' that had been commanding me in my dreams. Was I going to beg for my life now, like I had there?

Sarah got to her feet, and a deep, primal part of me felt the urge to mount her. To grab her body, throw her to the ground, and take her like a bitch in heat. It took all my willpower to resist the urge. It wasn't me; it had to be the influence of the presence before us.

She ran forwards, arms open. Just before she reached one of the tentacles, the Minotaur came out of nowhere, and charged. It grabbed onto the tentacle closest to Sarah and pulled, ripping it from the core. The beak snapped closed, cutting off the deep sound that rumbled through the air. I was confused. Wasn't the Minotaur its servant?

An example must be made. Witness.

Several of the smaller tentacles whipped out and wrapped around the Minotaur, effectively immobilizing it, as well as lifting it, as though displaying it for our benefit. More tentacles slithered over the body, until only the head was exposed. One tentacle moved over the skull and pulled, yanking it free with the sound of tearing skin and sinew.

At first I thought the tentacle was ripping the Minotaur's head off, but then I saw that it was some sort of mask that had become embedded in the skin around its neck. Now that the skull had been removed I got a clear view of the face underneath, and my mind went blank.

"No! NO!" It was *my* face hidden under the skull. My...the Minotaur's eyes were bloodshot, and looked frenzied. It stared at me, but did nothing else.

Defiance leads to madness. Witness, David.

The tentacles squeezed, tight and hard, crushing him. The Minotaur made no noise, nor did its gaze leave mine as a fountain of blood began to gush forth, splashing onto the ground below. Once the Minotaur was dead, the tentacles shoved the ruined corpse into the beak. I could hear the bones crunch as the creature bit down.

Serve. One way, or another.

I bolted upright, panting heavily. My body was covered in a cold sweat and I realized that I had dreamt the whole thing. Had I? I looked around and saw that I was still in the clearing, but Victoria and Irene were both gone. I wanted to call out for them, but it was dark, and I didn't want to draw attention to myself. Where had they gone? Victoria was capable, but I doubted she could carry Irene for very long. It made no sense.

I thought back to the dream. To *who* the Minotaur had been. Was it just fear affecting my imagination, or would I actually somehow become the thing that hunted us? Had I said something in my sleep that had scared off the other two?

I stood on shaky legs, trying to orient myself. I wiped the sweat from my face and took in a deep breath, letting it out slowly. The last thing we had spoken about was going back to the mall. Maybe trying to find the panic room.

I took off in what I thought was the right direction, hoping I would bump into Victoria and Irene sooner rather than later.

I didn't see another living soul on my way back to the mall. Everything looked exactly as we had left it, but the night sky had gotten darker. The exterior lights were the only source of illumination, and they barely lit the entrance.

I could still see the damage from the Minotaur bursting through the wall, and tried to find any signs that it might be nearby. Nothing seemed to be out of the ordinary, but I knew not to trust anything in this place. I sat, and I waited. One minute turned into five. Still no movement or signs of life from the mall. Satisfied that it was actually safe, I stepped from my hiding spot in the forest and out into the open.

I suddenly felt torn about what to do: should I continue into the mall, or turn and run back into the forest? As much as it terrified me, I couldn't shake the feeling that the mall wasn't just the center of all of this, but the solution to it as well. That it would somehow be what got me back home. It could have been no more than wishful thinking, but I honestly didn't care. The notion helped to ease my troubled mind and I continued forward.

As I got closer to the ruined entrance, the sound of glass crunching underfoot pierced the silence like a gunshot. I stopped, flinching, and tried to hear any other signs of life or movement. Nothing.

Taking in a quick breath to calm my nerves, I moved through the destroyed doorway and back into the mall. There was still no sign of the women, or anything else. Frowning a bit, I tried to orient myself, to figure out where I needed to go to get to the basement. I had to find the panic room.

I heard footsteps coming in my direction, but I couldn't see anyone. I glanced around, trying to find a place to hide, and decided to duck into a nearby shoe store. I managed to get behind the counter just as the footsteps stopped near the store entrance.

"The split was only supposed to make a single copy of everyone still stuck in the mall. There's been *three* of David so far."

It was a woman's voice. One I'd never heard before. Was she somehow involved in whatever was going on?

"Does it matter? He's keeping the subject occupied. We have more important things to worry about."

Randall. The son of a bitch sounded calm, collected. But what did he mean by subject?

"I still don't like this. The project has gone sideways, and we've lost all control. I don't want to die in this shitty mall, Randall."

"I run this project, and everything *is* going according to plan."

"But *I'm* the one who funded it, along with your son, and things are getting worse. Already his *and* your copies are dead, and I watched *my* copy die right in front of me! How much longer until it's finished, Randall?"

This was shedding new light on things, but it still didn't explain a lot. At least it confirmed that Randall wasn't just capitalizing on what had happened to the mall, he was fucking behind it.

"Keep your voice down. If the skinless husks show up we'll have to make a break for the panic room."

There was a pause before the woman spoke. "Well?"

"Well what?"

"What's the code? My first visit to the site and all of *this* happens. *Christ.*"

"Not here."

"Who the fuck is going to hear us? The women are in the food court, as good as dead, and, according to you, the other David is still outside."

There was another pause, and Randall sighed. "Eleven, twenty, eighty six."

"That's your son's birthday! The amount I funneled into this, and you pull sentimental *bullshit* for the security code?"

"It doesn't matter." The annoyance was growing in his voice. I desperately wanted to peek over the counter to see them, but I stayed motionless, hoping they would just hurry up and leave. Now that I had the code, I could get into the panic room. I also knew where Victoria and Irene were.

"Whatever. Come on. There's one last place to look for *our* Reggie before we finish all this."

There was no reply, so I assumed that Randall must have nodded in agreement. I waited a few minutes after the sound of their footsteps faded away before I poked my head out from behind the register counter. The coast was clear.

I took in a breath and let it out as I walked out into the mall. I looked in the direction of the food court, and decided that if Victoria and Irene had made it this far, they were probably going to be okay. I told myself that if they managed to find their way to the panic room after I did, I'd let them in. A feeble attempt to justify abandoning them.

It was flimsy reasoning, but *they* left me outside. It could have been a conscious decision, or just a reaction to something I had said or done in my sleep. Hell, there was no guarantee that they'd even want me around if we met up again.

I looked in the opposite direction, and wondered how in the hell I was going to find my way to a lower level when I could barely navigate the one I was on? It wasn't going to be on any of those damned maps, that was for sure. Feeling vulnerable, I ducked back into the shop and got back behind the counter. No sense standing out in the open; I could think much better if I was safe in my hiding spot.

As I sat there pondering what to do, I saw a door leading to a back area of the shop. I wasn't sure why, but a strange urge overtook me and I got up and went inside. Shutting the door behind me, I fumbled in the dark for the light switch, and blinked rapidly in the sudden brightness when I found it. It was a small storage area, but there was a set of double doors on the far wall. I continued to follow that strange urge, and crossed to them. It didn't feel like a surprise when I found that they were unlocked.

I stepped through to a well lit service hallway. It looked like something I had seen in a movie once. Was that what pushed me forward? Some long forgotten memory? It didn't matter. Now, at least, I could find my way to safety. I turned left and walked down the hall until I came to a sign. It indicated that access to the lower level was in the opposite direction, so I turned around and made my way quickly back the way I had come. For once, things were starting to look up.

*****

It wasn't long before I was lost in the maze of tunnels underneath the mall. I had passed a map when I first entered the area, but it was so technical that trying to sort out the path from the plumbing and electrical grids had given me a headache. Besides, I couldn't see anything on it that indicated any sort of room, panic or otherwise.

My intuition and faded memories could only get me so far. I was making yet another left hand turn, probably going in circles, when I heard footsteps. Were Randall and the mystery woman here already? I frantically looked around for some place to hide, but options were slim. I finally managed to squeeze behind a very warm pipe on the wall and froze, holding my breath.

Victoria came into view, carrying Irene. I hesitated, wondering if I should remain hidden, but decided that even if they had left me, we were all here now and we had better chances of staying alive if we were in a group. I slipped from behind the pipe, grateful that it was no longer roasting my crotch.

"You two look lost," I joked.

Victoria swung around and stuck me, hard, right in the temple. She moved so quickly that she dropped Irene on her ass. The world went black for a second, then pain bloomed right behind my eyes. I cried out and dropped to a knee, hissing at them.

"What the fuck?!"

"D-David?!"

I looked up at her, and saw the genuine shock on her face. Then she ran up and hugged me, tight.

"We watched you *die*."

"How?" There was no surprise in my voice. Just an hour ago I had discovered that I was some sort of anomaly in this place. Anything they said would probably be the truth. At the very least, it confirmed they hadn't just left me.

"I had watch, and dozed off," Irene stated. "We both woke up to the sound of...*god*. I can't even describe it. Something was hunched over you, and the two of us got out of there as fast as we could."

"We figured that if we could find the panic room, we might be able to brute force our way through the door or something," Victoria added.

"But, the thing...did you actually see it attacking me, or was it just hunched over?"

They looked at each other, and realization spread across their faces. Victoria brought a hand to her mouth and her eyes began to well up. "Jesus. It was so dark, we couldn't tell."

I furrowed my brow, and decided they needed to know about the dream. "I don't know how to explain it, but I don't think what you saw was real."

Victoria took a step back, and Irene sat up, leaning against the wall, glaring at me. "What do you mean, David?"

"I had a dream where this...*presence* was trying to control me. It was trying to get me to serve it. In the dream, I was the Minotaur. I think somehow I'm going to *become* that thing chasing us."

"Bullshit," Irene spat out, and shook her head. "Even if you *were* becoming something dangerous, that thing is out there *now*."

Victoria and I looked at one another. I could tell from the way she was staring at me that she remembered Alex's theories about dimensions. What she didn't know, and what I had only recently discovered, was that there were multiple 'copies' of me. God only knew how many.

"I don't know for sure, but I think there's something powerful that lives in this place. Something with the power to manipulate space and time. It kept telling me that I was going to serve. That all would serve."

"Lives in the mall?" Irene's skeptical tone was beginning to annoy me. Hadn't she seen the same sort of things that Victoria and I had?

"If you don't believe me, after all the insanity and horror that we've seen, fine. The mall isn't in the same city anymore. Fuck, it isn't even in the same world. Dimension! Whatever! We're probably going to die in that panic room if we ever find it. But it seems like that may be the only place where that thing can't get to me!"

I couldn't hide the terror in my voice. They hadn't seen it. Hadn't gazed upon its impossible form, or watched as it ate their own ruined corpses. I was only thinking of myself, and it showed. Victoria frowned slightly, and paused for a moment before she replied.

"It doesn't matter if we find it since we can't open it."

"I have the code."

"How did you get that?" Irene ignored my hand as I offered to help her up onto my back.

"I overheard Randall and and some woman talking about it. He's been a part of this since the beginning. I don't even know if he's a real doctor."

"Who was the woman?"

I didn't have time to explain, so I ignored Irene's question and turned to Victoria. "We need to find that room and lock ourselves in. I don't know what that presence is trying to do to me, or why, but I want to get as far away from it and its influence as possible. If I start going crazy in the room, just kick me out. Okay?"

I sounded desperate, but I couldn't shake the feeling in the back of my mind that no matter where I went, this thing had its claws deep in my flesh, and wasn't about to let me go.

"Fine. You carry Irene, my back is sore. We'll figure out what to do next *if* we can find the damn room."

I nodded in agreement and Irene let me help her onto my back. She wrapped her arms around my neck and leaned into whisper, "I won't throw you out. I'll just kill you." I swallowed and gave a curt nod as we continued through the basement.

Time seemed to drag as we searched and searched. Anything that looked unusual got a second glance, but there wasn't much. We encountered far too many dead ends for my liking, and had even wound up going in circles a few times. Was it just because we were unfamiliar with the layout, or was it an intentional part of Randall's design?

I was beginning to feel like Theseus, but I quickly pushed the comparison out of my head. The last thing we needed down here was the Minotaur. In the cramped space, with no idea where we were or where we needed to go, there was no way we could get away from it.

"Another dead end."

Victoria's voice was devoid of all emotion. I looked at her face, and saw how emotionally and physically exhausted she was. There were dark circles under her eyes and I wondered if she had gotten any sleep over the past couple of days. Had it actually *been* days? Or just hours? It was impossible to tell.

"We have to keep looking."

"We don't even know what we're looking for! I say we just get out of this fucking basement and hide somewhere in the mall. At least up there we can run."

There was logic to Irene's statement, but I didn't want to give up. We were so goddamn close...it was frustrating.

"No. We keep looking. It's a panic room, right? Which means it's supposed to be hidden. We need to look differently."

Irene rolled her eyes at me. Or, at least, I assumed she did, judging from the scoffing sound that escaped her lips. Victoria just looked at me. Rather, she looked *through* me, and walked past. She was resigned to dying down here, whether it happened in the halls or in the panic room.

About twenty minutes later we had finally made our way back to the map next to the entrance. I put Irene down and tried to rub the pain out of my shoulders. She wasn't making it easy to carry her, and I was getting more than a little annoyed with her attitude. At least the other Irene had been more agreeable before her death.

Victoria was engrossed with going over every inch of the map, her fingers gliding softly across the lines of each pipe, each drawn schematic. She was going down one side when her fingers stopped and she quirked an eyebrow.

"Find something?" The spot her finger was resting on didn't look special. Just a hallway where several junctions, both plumbing and electric, met.

"Look at all the other hallways. Everything is, mostly, in a straight line. Fuse boxes and the like are in dead ends. But here?" She tapped her finger. "There's a lot of odd things here.

T-sections that lead nowhere. Elbow joints. Dead space. But...there's no way this is a panic room. There's not enough room. There's another hallway just on the other side."

"You can understand this?"

"My father was a contractor. I used to look over blueprints with him all the time. They fascinated me."

"Must have been some guy."

She didn't say anything, just frowned slightly. I decided not to push it. Last thing I wanted was repressed family issues bubbling to the surface.

"I say we check it out." I shrugged. "It's not too far from here, and since you can read this better than I can, we can find our way back easily enough, right?"

She nodded and I knelt down to help Irene onto my back again, when a scream came from the top of the stairs. It was Sarah.

"FEAST! FEAST!!"

"Jesus, she's gonna-" Irene never finished her sentence, because the Minotaur burst through the door, throwing Sarah against the wall. She didn't get back up, and it barely glanced in her direction.

"Move, now!!"

"What if we're wrong?!"

"We don't have a choice!"

I didn't bother with hoisting Irene onto my back, just carried her like a toddler down the hall, following Victoria. There were several twists and turns, and I started to wonder if she actually knew the way. The Minotaur thundered down the stairs and I heard it slam into the wall, bursting several pipes as it did. The sound of escaping steam filled the air as Victoria skidded to a stop in front of a wall.

"This...this is it, but..:"

"But what? Fucking open the door, bitch!" When Irene called Victoria a bitch, I thought about just throwing her back at the Minotaur, but I decided against it.

"There's nothing here! No panel, no keypad...it's just a wall!"

She was right. There was nothing on the wall that would indicate something was hidden behind it. Maybe she had read the map wrong. Maybe she just assumed too much. I didn't blame her, really. The pressure of this place had finally gotten to her. I looked back down the hall just as the Minotaur stepped into view. It wasn't rushing any more, just taking its time. It knew we were trapped.

I noticed an electrical box on the wall, just to the left of where Victoria was standing. I reached over and tried to pull it open, but it was locked.

Victoria saw me messing around with it and her eyes grew wide. I didn't care that she hadn't seen it. All I cared about was breaking it open and getting to safety. She rushed over to try and help me pry it open as the Minotaur almost casually made his way down the hall.

"Use my knife!" Irene yelled, shoving a pocket knife into the space between us. Victoria took it and slid it under the box's door. She leaned all her weight against it and managed to break it open, cutting her hand in the process but exposing the keypad.

"One-one, two-zero, eight-six!" I yelled, and she quickly typed it in. Nothing happened.

"Try it again!" Irene yelled, and Victoria quickly punched in the numbers. Again, nothing happened.

"I thought you knew the code!" Victoria yelled, holding her bleeding hand. It didn't make sense. Those were the numbers, exactly as Randall had said them. Had he lied to that other woman? Was that ultimately going to be what fucking killed us? *A simple lie?*

In my frustration, I slammed my fist into the panel. There was the sound of something shorting out, and a spark, then a the wall to the right of us slid open. I heard the Minotaur scream and start to run as we entered. The doors slid closed just before it reached us, leaving us in darkness. The sound of it beating on the door reverberated around us as it tried to get inside.

The lights flickered on and we saw that we were in what seemed to be an elevator, but one without buttons. Soft music filled the air as we started to descend.

"Where the hell are we going?"

Victoria slid down the wall until she was sitting on the floor. I wondered the same thing. Maybe the panic room was far more protected that we realized. But, somehow, I couldn't shake the feeling that we were beginning a descent into hell.

XVI

It was impossible to tell how fast the elevator was moving, or how far down we'd actually gone. As well as having no buttons, there was no floor indicator or emergency phone. We remained silent, with only the buzzing of the light fixture and the hum of machinery to keep us company. Suddenly there was the screech of static feedback, making me wince, followed by a voice from nowhere. There must have been an intercom, but I couldn't see it.

"I'm surprised that you managed to get inside. What do you hope to find, David? Salvation? Safety? The man-made ideals providing comfort against the cold, dark night for those with weak wills and diminished intellect. You know the truth. You've seen it, just as I have."

It was Randall's voice, but he was only addressing me. He apparently had no idea that Victoria and Irene were in here with me. Maybe we could use that to surprise him, catch him off guard as the doors opened.

"I'm sure you're thinking of some way to attack me as soon as those doors open, but the sad truth is, I'm not down there. Don't worry, though. Where you're going is very, very *special*."

I looked over at Victoria and her face mirrored my own feelings. I didn't like the way he emphasized the final word. Nothing in this place was worthy of being called that.

"This is where it all began. I'd recommend not...*touching* anything."

There was a click, and the voice was gone. The buzz from the light somehow seemed louder than it had before.

"What's he talking about? What the *fuck* is your connection to all of this, David?" Irene was sitting on the floor,
arms crossed, looking up at me accusingly.

"I've already told you, I've got no goddamn idea *what*
the hell is going on here, *or* how I'm connected. Just that,
somehow, I am."

"I don't buy it." She pointed a finger at me. I was sure
that, were we eye to eye, she would have been jabbing it into
my chest. "There's a lot of shit going down here, David. First,
you die, *several times*. Then you tell us that you've been having
these weird fucking dreams where you're one of the things trying to kill us. And now? Now you have the *gall* to play dumb?
Fuck you. I don't trust you."

I glared at her, but she was right. There was every indication that I was somehow wrapped up in everything that was
going on, and absolutely no way to prove that I wasn't. I leaned
back against the cold steel wall of the elevator and closed my
eyes, sighing.

"I don't know what else to tell you, other than *I. Don't.
Know.*" I spat the words, frowning.

I heard Irene scoff, but there was no further argument.
I opened my eyes and saw Victoria leaning over her, whispering into her ear. Fine, if they both wanted to distrust me, then
that's their prerogative. I just wanted to wake up from this
nightmare.

I moved away from the wall and crossed to stand in
front of the door. We'd been descending for about five minutes
now, and I had a feeling we were nearing the end of the trip. I
couldn't put my finger on it, but I could *feel* something the further down we went. It reminded me of the buzz of the light, but
this was something I felt instead of heard.

Thirty seconds later, the doors slid open. There were no
lights on in the room outside, but enough light spilled from the
elevator that I could see, and I gasped in surprise. I don't know
what I had been expecting, but this looked more like an office
than a panic room. There were desks with computers arranged
neatly around the room, and large servers lined one of the far
walls. There were a few other doors, as well as a large bay window on the wall to the right. The room beyond the window was
dark, but I could see the faint outline of some strange device.

I took a step forward and felt Victoria grab my arm, hard. I turned back to her and she stared at me in surprise.

"What is it?"

"You're seriously going out into that mess? What if something's hiding?"

"Mess? What are you-"

I turned back to the room, and it had changed from neat and proper to something that looked like a tornado had passed through. Desks were overturned, half of the servers were burned out, and paper and debris littered the floor. The bay window was broken, with only a few shards of glass remaining in the frame. The strange device from the next room was missing as well. In its place was some sort of strange, organic mass.

"But...but this was..." There was no doubt, now. I had to be going mad. Or was this another vision, something shown to me by that creature I kept encountering? They had never happened while I was awake before though, and the idea that they might be now was terrifying. If I couldn't discern fiction from reality...

"We need to be cautious. Irene, you should stay in here, just in case." Victoria warned.

"And let the elevator take me back upstairs to the bull fuck? No. No fucking thank you. You wanna play detective, go ahead. I'll just crawl behind a desk or something."

I pulled away from Victoria's grip and stepped out of the elevator. I was only fifteen feet or so into the room when a faint odor hit me. It reminded me of a compost heap. I immediately thought of my grandmother, working in her garden, singing long-forgotten songs from her youth as she hunched over, pulling out weeds and tending to her flowers.

It was such a powerful recall. I felt as if I were there, standing next to her.

"Hand me that brugmansia shrub, David." She didn't turn to face me, just continued to work in the dirt, digging a spot out for the bush. "It's right next to the daturas."

Everything seemed off about the memory. The plants weren't right...she planted roses and tulips. These sounded...odd. I tried to remember where I'd heard such names before.

"Come on, David, you little pussy. Pass me the goddamn plant."

This wasn't my memory. It couldn't be. My grandmother was a sweet, kind- "Your grandmother was a fucking whore who spread her legs for any cock that she could find." She turned to me, her warm, gentle features twisted into a snarl as she pointed at me with her trowel. "I sucked cock, David. Right behind Granddad's back. I sucked and fucked and made enough money on my back to buy this garden. The place I fucking buried him! TURN AWAY, DAVID! SERVE! SERVE!!"

She lunged at me then, and I raised my arms, crying out in surprise. When I felt someone grab me, I tried to fight them off.

"David! Stop it!" It was Victoria. I took a few deep breaths, trying to reorient myself, and shook my head.

"I told you we couldn't trust him," Irene said from off to the side.

"It was another dream, wasn't it? But...you were awake this time."

I just nodded. I hadn't even registered when it had changed from a random memory to something far more visceral. This thing had its hooks into me far deeper than I had realized. I glanced around the ruined room, until my eyes fell on the broken window. Something was in there. Something I needed to see.

"See if you can find a light. I need to look at something."

Victoria seemed a bit put off by my request, but she complied. I felt like there were answers just beyond my grasp, and the only way I was going to get them was to see what was inside that room. The compost smell grew stronger the closer I got to the broken window. It wasn't overpowering, but it was enough to make me cover my nose.

"I think this is the light." I heard a switch flip, and the lights came on, but only in the room beyond the window. It was so bright I had to turn away, blinking rapidly to help my eyes adjust.

"WHAT THE FUCK IS THAT?!" Irene's voice was filled with terror.

I already knew before I turned to look. A part of me had known the moment I stepped out of the elevator and the odor hit me. There in the side room, in advanced stages of decay, was the thing from my dreams. The terrible dark god.

It was much smaller than I had envisioned it originally. The one in the woods had been massive, big enough to eat the Minotaur in a couple bites. The husk lying in front of me now was the size of a large horse. It looked desiccated; its tentacles were dried out, and the giant eye that its beak extended from was milky white and slightly shriveled. A thick black tongue lolled out of its mouth. It had to be the source of the stench; it was the only thing in the room, aside from a ruined device that I couldn't identify.

I had never described the thing to either of the women, so I made a choice to keep it from them now. If they knew that this was the thing in my dreams, there was no telling how they would react. How they would react towards *me*.

"It's dead, whatever it is." I replied to Irene's terrified question. "From the looks of it, it's been dead for a while."

"That thing seem familiar? Or anything else in here? Randall said you'd 'understand', whatever that meant." Victoria was still standing over by the switch.

I just shrugged. "No, nothing familiar, and I don't understand shit about this." I turned away from the creature, and made my way over to a door near the server wall.

"Wait, is there light coming from that door?"

I stopped walking and looked where Irene was pointing. I hadn't noticed light coming from underneath that door before, so maybe it had come on when Victoria flipped the switch. I made my way there instead.

"I don't like this. We need to get out of here, find another way back to the basement without that Minotaur seeing us." Victoria's pleas may as well had fallen onto deaf ears. I was compelled to open the door.

Turn away.

It was in my head, whispering quietly to me, trying to get me to ignore this new path. Was this the way out? Was this what we needed? It had to be. Why else would it be trying so hard to get me to *not* open the door?

"Get the fuck out of my head." I said under my breath, flinging the door open. A far more powerful, and horrible, stench filled my nostrils and I began to gag. There was nothing in my stomach to throw up, but I dry heaved and fell to my knees.

I heard both Victoria and Irene vomit behind me, and I turned back towards the room, my eyes stinging from the stench.

It was just an empty storage closet, but there was a body nailed to the far wall. Symbols and runes were written on the walls and floor in blood, but it was so old that it had turned black. I didn't recognize any of them, but just looking at them filled me with primal fear and dread. I wanted nothing more than to turn away and run, to find a hole to crawl into and hide.

The body had been completely skinned, except for the head. The body cavity was empty, so I assumed the gooey mass at its feet was the putrefied guts. The face was unrecognizable in its current state, the gray skin barely hanging onto the skull.

I quickly shut the door, gasping for breath, but that only made me gag again; the smell had gotten into my throat, and I could taste it. I scrambled back to the middle of the room, coughing and spitting.

"Do you understand now, David?" Randall's mocking voice filled the room. "Of course you don't. You're as stupid as the rest of them. An anomaly and a curiosity...but still cattle to the slaughter. This room is what started it all, and this room is where it will all end. For you."

Sacrifice. Cut the bitch.

"No! NO!" I screamed, pounding my fists on the cold, hard floor. I looked for Victoria and Irene, but only saw Victoria, curled up into a ball. It was no surprise that she had regressed; it was a wonder *I* was still cognizant of my surroundings. Irene, however, wasn't where she had been.

The elevator doors were still wide open, and she clearly wasn't in there. I heard glass crunch by the broken window and saw her *crawling* through it. I tried to stand, to stop her, but a pain went through my head and made me feel as though it were splitting apart.

YES. SERVE. CUT THE BITCH IN HALF.

"I-Irene!" I called out after her, but it was no use. She was climbing through the broken window, and I could see the remaining shards of glass cutting into her skin as she made her way over. Crying out in agony, I forced myself to stand and move towards her. If I could just grab her, pull her back...

She fell over the sill into the room. I stumbled forward, using the overturned desks for support as I crossed the room. I grabbed onto the window frame, ignoring the minor cuts from the glass and couldn't believe what I was seeing.

Irene was stripping out of her clothes, smearing the blood from her wounds all over herself. Once she was completely naked, she continued to crawl towards the dead thing in the corner.

"Serve. All serve. Witness."

Whatever else she was saying became incoherent as she reached the beak. She positioned her arm so that it rested inside of it, then grabbed the top of the beak and looked right at me.

Smiling, she licked her lips and screamed, "WITNESS! SERVE!"

Then she brought the beak down, hard. I could see blood welling up from the new wounds.

"Stop it! You're killing her!!"

She giggled with delight as she brought it down again and again, tearing up her flesh more and more. Blood poured from the wound as she continued to use the beak to 'chew' through her arm. Just as it seemed everything was almost over, she raised the beak high and let go. Her expression changed from frenzied and mad to one of stark realization. She looked down at her ruined arm and screamed. The thing had given her mind back to her.

"Oh...oh Jesus What the fuck...what the fuck?!"

The lights began to strobe and I felt a powerful, guttural bellow come from nowhere and everywhere at once. It was the same noise the god had made in my dream. I continued to watch in horror as the beak moved on its own, and continued to chew, moving to her torso. It seemed impossible, but she remained alive and aware as it continued its grisly task.

Tentacles came to life, wrapping around her and moving her body so her midsection was in line with the beak. With a sickening crack, it bit through her spine, and one of the dried out tentacles started to shove pieces of her lower body into its mouth. Irene tried to crawl away, coughing up blood and wailing as she did.

A tentacle wrapped around her neck, squeezing hard enough to make her eyes bulge as it pulled her back and finished consuming her. I couldn't turn away; it was mesmerizing.

Suddenly I was back in my grandmother's garden. "She served. Fed the garden. Brought it back."

"What...what do you want from me?"

"Serve. Either serve or feed the garden."

"I will never serve."

"Oh, my sweet little David. You already *have!*"

I looked over her shoulder to see what she was working on, and saw my face in the hole she had been digging. She took the trowel and stabbed it into my cheek. Black fluid quickly welled up to fill the hole.

"You serve *and* you feed. Such a wonderfully curious thing you are."

I was back in the ruined room. The creature and Irene were both gone, the only indication that anything had ever been in the room was a large pool of blood on the floor. I quickly looked around for Victoria, and breathed a sigh of relief when I saw her.

She was trembling as I helped her to her feet. I didn't want to go back up to the surface, and I certainly didn't feel comfortable in this room anymore, so I made my way over to one of the other doors and opened it, praying there wouldn't be another sacrifice inside.

XVII

I was relieved to discover that the door opened into a hallway, maybe fifty or sixty feet long. There were two doors on the right, one on the left, and one at the other end. Feeling slightly safer in this enclosed space, I leaned against a wall and took in a deep breath.

Randall was insane. Somehow, he'd had this facility built underneath the mall. But how? How long had the mall been here? I found I couldn't remember, but then, it didn't really matter. *How* this place existed didn't matter to me as much as *why* it existed. What was the end game? Obviously we were in some sort of research facility, but what was with the body and the runes in the closet?

Something dark and forbidden had happened here. But the fact that Randall seemed so calm, even after everything, told me one vital truth: there had to be a way out. There was no way someone went through all of this trouble without reason. That reason was still a mystery though, and one I didn't want to care about.

"Where's Irene?" I looked at Victoria and shook my head in response, unable to speak. She looked down at the floor and nodded softly, understanding. "We *are* going to die here."

"No. There's got to be a way out."

Her eyes met mine, but there was nothing there. Whatever light, whatever drive had been there was simply gone. She was beaten and broken, and had clearly given up. Why hadn't I? The question struck me to my core.

We were fighting so hard to try and get out, without any idea about whether or not it was even possible. Was Randall still the one in control? Or was it that thing that kept invading my mind and my dreams?

"There *has* to be," I reiterated. If nothing else, I had to convince myself.

Victoria looked away from me and then did something I didn't expect. She moved past me and tried one of the doors on the right, then the next, when the first was locked. The second door was unlocked, and she turned the knob and glanced inside. After a moment of inspection she turned back to me.

"Alright, David. Prove it. Get us out of here."

At least she was still willing to try. I guess when all hope runs out, the only motivation left is survival.

I had just taken a step towards her when the door on the left flew open and a figure ran out, slamming against the opposite wall before sliding to the floor.

"Shut it! Shut it now!!"

Without thinking I reached out and grabbed the door, pushing it closed just as something that moved with unnerving speed slammed into it. An angry roar followed, and whatever it was began trying to beat its way out. After trying, unsuccessfully, to break down the door there was one final thud before it finally gave up.

Victoria and I went to the figure on the floor. It was a man with dark hair, clean shaven, about thirty-five or forty. He was favoring his left arm. When I noticed he was wearing a lab coat, I saw red. Grabbing him by the collar, I lifted him up roughly and slammed him into the wall, causing him to wince in pain.

"What the *fuck* is going on here?! What have you people done??"

He began to stutter as he tried to defend himself with his good arm. "M-m-my n-name is T-T-Timothy Renton. I'm an assis-s-s-stant here. Look, I only know that s-something went wrong, *very* wrong, about thirty minutes ago."

His stutter faded as he calmed down, until finally disappearing completely. I stared at him, wanting to strangle the life out of him, but instead I let him go and turned away, slamming my fist against the wall. The thing behind the door responded by hitting something as well.

"It has been *days* since this all began, not just thirty minutes," Victoria tried to clarify.

"That's impossible. The accident *just* happened!"

I thought it would take too long to try and explain what was going on, considering the pocket dimensions and mysterious clones, so I decided to start by hearing his version of things. "What accident?"

I moved to stand next to Victoria, and Timothy shook his head as he began to tell his story.

"At the behest of the director-"

'Who? What's his name?"

Timothy looked up at us and squinted his eyes as he really saw us for the first time. "Wait, who the hell are you? I don't recognize either of you."

I was going to keep my mouth shut, but Victoria volunteered the information. "My name is Victoria, and this is David. We're from the mall."

Timothy shut his eyes tightly and let out a sigh. "Jesus, this is worse than I calculated. This is an *omega* event." Opening his eyes again, he asked, "How different is it topside?"

She took the next few minutes to describe the condition of the mall and the surrounding area, and the creatures that stalked the corridors. Timothy seemed genuinely interested, but not terrified. It was unnerving. Perhaps it was the scientist in him. Perhaps not.

"This is *incredible*! We only anticipated a low-level containment breach. Nothing large enough to..."

His voice trailed off as the wheels in his head began to turn, then his eyes went wide and he brushed past us, going back to the room at the bottom of the elevator. Tentatively, I followed him.

"Shit. *Shit!*"

"What is it?"

"We managed to acquire a creature. We had it under observation through that glass but it looks like it somehow managed to revive and escape."

"Why does it matter?"

"Because that creature has abilities. Abilities we could use and manipulate before things went sideways. It was critical to the success of our experiments."

"What experiment? What are you people doing here? And who the fuck is your director?"

"It's...complicated. The best way I can describe this place is as a kind of purgatory. Hell, that's our code word for it. It's a place *between* places; dimensions. Only instead of there being separate spaces between each different dimension, there's one *central* space. Like the hub of a wheel. Our goal was to explore that in-between space and see if it could be used to travel between dimensions in a stable fashion."

"Huh. So Alex was right."

"Who's Alex?"

"He was part of the group that got trapped in the mall when all this started. He suspected alternate dimensions," Victoria answered, as she moved into the room and stood next to me. "I didn't like being alone in that hallway."

I couldn't blame her, not with whatever that thing was trapped in the other room.

"So, what happened here?" I probed again.

Timothy attempted to mess around with one of the few terminals that was still intact. "To be perfectly honest, I don't know. We were running another incursion..." He glanced up. He must have sensed our confusion, because he took a minute to explain. "That's what we call our trips between Purgatory and other dimensions." Then he went on. "Everything was routine. But, we lost track of the team and something got through, outside of containment. In my perception of time it's only been about half an hour."

"Your perception?"

"We discovered that when travelers get separated, time starts to move differently. Sometimes it's only off by a few minutes, sometimes by hours, or even *days*. At first we thought it was only affecting individuals, but then we realized that it was affecting whole groups, provided they remained in relatively close proximity."

The monitor flickered to life, a blinking cursor awaiting input. Timothy grinned wide, and pulled over a chair as he brushed debris off the keyboard. "Perfect! Now I can see exactly what's happened, and what the extent of the damage is."

"Timothy...that creature...it got into my head." Maybe he could tell me how to keep it out.

"Impossible. While in full containment, it's unable to influence living creatures."

"What about dead ones?"

He stopped for a moment and shrugged. "Explains those things you've been fighting. Masses of dead cells that it was able to control through some type of telekinesis. We've been exploring Purgatory for months, but we have never seen anything like what you described."

I recalled how it told me that I served it *and* fed it. Maybe it had something to do with the fact that there were apparently more than two of me running around this place. I was just wondering if I should tell him about *that* anomaly, when the screen flashed red.

"*Fuck*. This is...it's impossible. Completely impossible. None of the equipment we have here is capable of opening a fracture - that's what we call the doorways into other dimensions - more than five feet large. Ten feet tops. This one engulfed the entire mall and dropped it into Purgatory. But...it..."

He was hesitating, as if some great truth had been put before him and he was rebelling against it. "It what? What aren't you telling us?"

"This wasn't an accident. This was done intentionally, from the director's office."

"You know that for certain?"

"Guess she didn't anticipate anyone being alive, or she didn't care. Every time a fracture is opened, it's logged, no matter how small. Where it was initiated from, how long it lasted, what went through it...Dozens of variables, all recorded. This was an intentional overload started from the director's computer."

"She?!"

Before I could question him further, Victoria spoke up. "Is there any way to reverse it?!" Her voice was filled with hope. I decided to forgo the rest of my questions when I saw the tiniest of twinkles glimmering in her eyes. The director's identity suddenly didn't matter. Her hope was infectious, and I prayed that Timothy would say there was.

"I have no idea. This is all unprecedented. We only ever ventured *through* the in-between space, never remaining within it more than a few minutes. But there were always safety measures; tethers, emergency generators, ways to get back.

The whole goddamn mall was transported, and *none* of those were in place. Also...there is no set 'home beacon.' We had to always extrapolate that relative to whatever dimension we wanted to travel to. We never had to do it from *inside* purgatory. There's no way to know if a designated location would be correct."

"It's better than this hell. We've got to at least try."

"I can't say I disagree with you, but most of the equipment is back in the room I just escaped from. That thing busted up my arm pretty good, as well as some of the components. If we want to try, we have to get past it."

Okay, at least we now had a plan. It wasn't the greatest plan, but it was hope, and hope was more than we'd had since this whole mess started. We might have a way out of here. A nagging doubt popped into the back of my mind, and I decided to ask Timothy about it.

"We're currently linked with another dimension, right?"

He looked at the screen, typed a few commands, and furrowed his brow. "Sort of. Dimensions are odd things, when all is said and done. They can lay on top of one another, like pieces of paper, only they all take up the same space at the same time. It looks like this fracture pulled two different dimensions into the same spot, mixing them. It's highly possible that different areas of the mall are acting as direct conduits between them."

"So, at most, there should be two versions of each of us running around? If that?"

He nodded. "Exactly. When we started this experiment, fear and a desire for safety led us to select a dimension very nearly identical to our own. I think the only significant difference we discovered was that the guy from *Where's Waldo* wears red stripes instead of purple!" He laughed at his own joke, but his eyes grew wide in fascination when Victoria and I didn't join in.

"My god, you're *from* the other dimension! Or, maybe *I* am. This is fascinating! We thought the one we went to didn't have a lab like this one, but maybe they just built it in a different location."

"Look, that's not my point. What if there were more than two of a person? Three, four, maybe more. What would that mean?"

Timothy looked confused for a moment, then shook his head. "No. That's just not possible. I *know* it's not. That would mean that more dimensions were linked, but then there'd be multiples of *everyone*, not just a single person. A refraction isn't something that we were ever able to create, nor did we witness it occurring naturally during any of our trips."

"Refraction?"

"What you've described, we had a theory about that...called it a refraction." He stopped for a moment and seemed deep in thought. "It's like this: when light is put through a prism, it gets split into its base colors, but each color is still *fundamentally* light. The only way that a refraction could be possible is if a person experienced that same prism effect when put through the fracture."

"What if I told you I've seen several copies of myself. Watched one die."

"I'd laugh in your face, because you're clearly delusional."

"He has. I've seen it too."

I looked over at Victoria. Had she really seen more, or did she trust me enough to fudge the truth so that Timothy would trust me as well? I gave her a small smile of thanks.

Timothy's brow furrowed again as he looked from me to her and back again. Finally he shrugged. "Whenever presented with an impossible situation, accept it as truth until facts prove otherwise."

"Who said that?"

"My father. Okay, for the time being, I'll believe you. This might also explain why that thing was able to communicate with you. If you died, you'd be linked to it. Well, the duplicate would be, I...guess? If you are truly a refraction, then it's like a *part* of you died. Not another dimension's version; part of the *real* you. But honestly, that's the least of our concerns right now."

"What's more concerning than any of what you just told me?"

"Someone is in the director's office right now, accessing the same files that I am."

XVIII

We all stood there, looking at the screen in stunned silence. At first, I didn't know *what* to make of what Timothy had just said. The statement just hung in the air, and I furrowed my brow as my brain tried to decipher it, as though he spoke in another language.

"Someone else is down here with us? But isn't that," I motioned to the elevator, "the only way down?"

"It is. So that means they've been here since before you showed up."

"Maybe they arrived after we went into the hall?" Victoria spoke up, her eyes never leaving the screen.

"No, we would have seen them. The office is *in* that hallway where we met. Besides, this facility isn't exactly huge. There's just a few more research and equipment rooms."

"Can you tell what they're doing? Or who it is?"

"Not exactly." Timothy started to work on the keyboard, tapping keys sporadically. It was nothing like what I was used to seeing in movies, where all ten fingers were blazing. These were methodical, decisive keystrokes. A few more and he shook his head. "Nope. All I can tell is that, whoever they are, they're using the director's computer. The login isn't one I recognize. It could be anyone. And as for *what* they're doing..."

His voice trailed off as he continued to work the keyboard. The screen flashed a few times, and he soon became completely engrossed in whatever information he was getting. I looked over at Victoria, just as she glanced up at me. She offered a weak smile, but I wasn't sure if it was for my benefit or for her own.

"Ah!" Timothy's exclamation grabbed our attention, but I saw the corners of his mouth curl downwards into a frown. "Shit. They're shadow browsing."

"That...doesn't sound like a real term." Victoria's voice was filled with doubt and skepticism. I had to admit, I knew little about computers, but it did sound made up, even to my uneducated ears.

"It's not. Just what I'm calling it. As long as we have clearance, we can usually see logs from the entire system; what logins were used and when, what files each one accessed, how long they were in the files, and so on. But this just shows a user in the system. It shows when they logged on," he pointed at a time and date on the screen, "and the the folder they're in...but nothing more."

"What folder are they in?" My curiosity was piqued.

"Nothing critical, at the moment. Just records from the failed attempts to open fractures." He stopped for a moment, clicked a few more keys, and shook his head. "No, wait. Now they're accessing the camera system."

Timothy looked up at one corner of the room. There, a camera I hadn't noticed before turned to face us.

"Well. Smile everyone." He gave a mocking, sarcastic salute and I could only glare at the damn thing.

"We're going to that office," I snarled, and headed towards the door to the hallway.

"Wait!" Timothy called after me, but he didn't bother to get up.

Without turning around, I spoke to Victoria. "This may be the key to get out of here. If that's Randall, then we have a shot at this."

"Randall? Randall *Stiles??*" Timothy sounded surprised.

Now I turned around. "Yeah, the director, right?"

Timothy barked out a laugh and shook his head. "Jesus, *no*. Not officially, at any rate. His daughter-in-law, Gina, is the director."

I suddenly remembered I was going to grill him about this. The conversation I had overheard between her and Randall earlier now made *no* sense. Unless...Randall had found *her* copy? One that maybe wasn't the director? *Ugh*, I thought. *Trying to figure out this place is going to give me a aneurysm.*

"A few of us called Gina 'In Name Only' behind her back...especially when she started acting all haughty and bossy. Even though we only met him once, it was obvious that Randall actually ran the program through his funding. Seemed like a nice guy."

"He's anything but." The icy words slipped through Victoria's clenched teeth.

"We watched Randall and his son get killed...one of the first things that happened. Neither of them seemed to know what was going on here."

"Could be the truth, at least for those two. We tried to find a dimension close to our own, but there's no telling what could be different."

I didn't bother trying to put it all into a neat box. It would only make my headache worse. "Either way, we need to find out who's in that office. It could be the way out."

Timothy shook his head. "I'm staying right here. We don't know anything about what's going on in that office. Now that the creature is free, it can do whatever it wants. This could all be some elaborate illusion."

"It can do that?" Victoria took the words right out of my mouth. Timothy just nodded grimly.

"Fuck. I don't care. We have to try. Are you coming, or are you going to stay here with him?" I looked at Victoria. I would understand if she stayed behind, but I hoped she would join me. After a moment of hesitation, she nodded and crossed the room.

"I just want this to end." The spark was back in her eyes, and it filled me with the hope that we might be close to the end of our ordeal.

"Alright." I turned to Timothy, who was focused once again on the screen. "Can you see into the office?"

"No. That's the only place without a camera. Look, if things get hairy in there, I'm not going to save you. I'm going to find a place to hide, and try to get myself out."

I eyed the closet holding the human sacrifice, and decided not to tell him about it. If he wanted to be a coward, I figured he could discover that on his own. It was petty, but I was all out of tact. Victoria didn't tell him either, so I just turned away without a word and headed into the hallway.

It was almost exactly as we had left it. As we headed towards the door at the other end I noticed that the one Timothy had come out of was wide open. Gulping hard, I stopped and waited. If whatever had been chasing him was still in there, then the two of us were probably fucked.

But I wasn't about to let fear stop me. I stood right next to the door, reached inside, and fumbled around on the wall for a light switch. When I flipped it, the room was immediately bathed in fluorescent light.

I expected something to jump out at me the second I flipped the switch, but the thing, whatever it was, was dead. It looked like some large piece of equipment had fallen on it. Its upper body was underneath, and a large pool of thick, black blood surrounded it.

At first glance it looked humanoid with three legs. I leaned forward slightly to get a better look. Maybe two legs and one incredibly large...? It was hard to tell, and I wasn't about to get close enough to find out for sure. The skin was a blueish grey color, and heavily wrinkled. It looked dried out, and there were several small tentacles sticking out of its skin in a haphazard fashion.

"If it was killed in here, what opened the door?"

The implications of Victoria's question caused me to hyper analyze the room, coming up with dozens of scenarios. The most likely of which was that someone had come into the room from somewhere else., killed the creature, and then gone on into the office.

"Maybe...but how?"

"I don't know...through one of those...fracture things Timothy told us about?"

"But aren't they all controlled from here? How could one open from outside the room?"

"Maybe the same way the one opened in the woods?"

I had assumed that doorway was just a portal to another area of the mall, but what if it had been to another dimension? And even if it *had been* to someplace else within this purgatory, there had been no discernible way to control it. Plus, it had only showed up on a cube in the woods. *Not* inside the mall.

"Maybe. We just don-"

My words were cut off by a high-pitched whining noise. Something was revving to life in the far corner of the room. The lights dimmed slightly, then flickered back to full as the power usage leveled out and the whining became the low thrum of turning motors. A platform in the corner came to life, as something very similar to the doorway in the forest appeared.

Only, instead of an abandoned part of the mall, this time we could see people. Lots of them, going about their shopping and their lives as if nothing was amiss.

It was a portal home. It had to be.

"Oh...oh my god..." Victoria spoke no louder than a whisper, but there was awe and astonishment in her voice. She started to move towards it, but I grabbed her arm.

"Let go! We have to get in there before it closes!!"

"We don't know where that leads!"

"I don't care! It looks like paradise compared to this place."

Tears were streaming down her face, and I suddenly felt guilty and ashamed for stopping her. This place really was hell, and I was practically forcing her to stay but...why? Because I was too afraid? Too frightened to take the chance that salvation was just beyond that threshold?

"I can't stop you, but there's an old saying I can't get out of my head right now."

I knew that when I let go of her arm she would want to run for the fracture as fast as she could, but she stayed, asking, "What saying?"

"It's '*the devil will be attractive.*' Know what it means?" She shook her head. "It means that you should doubt anything that looks too good to be true. Because it probably is."

"And if you're wrong?" She was inching her way towards the portal, urging me to follow by holding out her hand.

Christ, this was hard. Or was it? I needed to make a decision, to either follow Victoria, or head to that office and get to the root of all of this. She kept heading towards the fracture, but something about it felt off. Even though the people seemed normal, and it looked like nothing was wrong, there was an odd haze over the setting. It was too...*yellow*.

I grabbed her hand again, but she yanked it away, her gaze boring into me.

"No, I'm not staying. Do whatever the hell you want, but I'm getting the fuck out of here."

"This isn't right. Can't you see that?!"

She spat out her reply. "If you're too afraid, that's your deal. When are we going to get another opportunity like this?!" She was practically in tears as she turned and, without another word, walked through the fracture.

It happened almost immediately. For a moment, the people in that dimension looked surprised that this woman in tattered, blood-stained clothing had suddenly appeared in the middle of their normal day at the mall. Then, Victoria doubled over, coughing and gasping for breath. Her eyes started to bulge and the veins on her neck began to pop out. Something was wrong, *very* wrong.

She began to shake violently, and a spatter of blood hit the floor with her next coughing fit. Cursing under my breath I reached through the portal, grabbed onto her, and pulled her back into the room. Even after being exposed for such a short time, I could feel my lungs and eyes burning. The stench of ammonia filled my nostrils as we both collapsed onto the floor.

Victoria started to cough again, gasping in ragged breaths as she rolled off of me. I sat up and started to check her over, trying to see if there was any permanent damage. The fracture closed.

"How...how did you know?" She managed to choke out, wiping the blood from her lips.

I could only shrug in return. "I didn't. It just didn't *look* right. We need to be more careful. There's no telling what could be on the other side of those things."

She nodded, and I could tell that she felt upset about being dismissive of my caution, but also thankful that I had been able to pull her back. I got up and waited for her to gain her composure, then helped her up as well.

"To the office then?"

I nodded and we exited the room. The closed door at the end of the hallway looked far more ominous than I remembered. There was no door knob, just a keypad on the side.

"Shit. I better go ask Tim for the code."

Victoria pushed on the door, and it swung open.

"No need." She didn't go in, though. It looked like I would be the one taking point on this. Steeling myself for whatever might happen, I walked inside.

The room itself was pretty standard looking, with a desk against the far wall, and the rest of the walls lined with bookcases. Various binders, books, specimen jars, and other research materials filled the shelves. The lights were off, and there was no one sitting at the desk. The glow from the monitor illuminated an empty chair. I looked around; there were no other doors in the room, so whoever had been in here had somehow gotten past us.

Immediately I was worried for Timothy's safety. 'Stay here." I told Victoria, and rushed back to the main room. Timothy was face down on the floor, a pool of blood quickly growing under him. I heard the ding of the elevator as the doors began to slide shut, and I dashed towards them, hoping to catch whoever was responsible. The face I saw, sporting a devilish grin, stopped me dead in my tracks. My jaw dropped as I immediately recognized it.

It was *my* face.

XIX

I closed my eyes. This was impossible. There was no way that could be me standing in the elevator. I had not just killed Timothy. None of my...my *refractions* could do such a thing, right? When I opened my eyes again, things felt different.

"You see, dear? It's so much easier now."

I turned around to see my grandmother, resting by her garden in a wooden chair. A glass of lemonade sat on the table next to her. She folded her arms and looked at me.

"Well, don't be rude. Come and sit. Let's chat."

I was suddenly sitting in a chair next to hers, a glass of lemonade in my hand, with no recollection of how I had gotten there. I knew none of this was real, but I took a sip; I couldn't help myself. It was exactly how she used to make it: far more tart than sweet. I had always hated my grandmother's lemonade.

"I could have changed this, you know. Made it all more pleasant than your own memories. Even convinced you it was real. But the time for subtlety is over. I felt a more overt demonstration was in order."

"Why are you doing this? What *are* you?"

"I am not a god, if that is what you're asking. Not even sure if I believe in such beings myself." She took her glass in hand and drank down half before putting it back on the table. "My, that *is* tart."

I stared at her, emboldened by the fact that it was approaching me like this. This was no dark vision, nor was it some dire message. *It was a goddamn conversation with the devil.* "Don't fucking ignore me. What the hell are you?"

"Mind your manners, *boy*. I have use of you, but I'm sure I can work around it if you become more trouble than you're worth."

"What use? How do I even know if anything that's been happening to me is real?"

"I can understand your doubts. My first attempts to engage you were...crude, at best."

"Engage? *Engage?!* You made me see and experience such...horrible things. You've burrowed your way into my head!"

The thing gussied up as my grandmother smirked. "All serve. At first I thought you a wonderful paradox. A being that both does and does not exist! Imagine my disappointment when I realized you were simply *broken*. Still, there are versions of you that I've got my tendrils in. You, however, are special."

"How so?"

"You're the original, of course! Using that scientist's crude description for the miracle gift you were given, *you* are the light that shone through the prism, creating all those wonderful copies. I especially like the brute."

"You're talking about the Minotaur, aren't you?"

She nodded. "He was incredibly easy to mold. Almost *too* easy. Compared to you, they all have been."

"You still haven't told me what you are, or why you want me so badly."

"Does one ever know one's self? Ha...you filthy bags of meat and water, hair and bone...coming up with such wonderfully convoluted philosophies and beliefs to explain something that is no more than a speck on the cosmic scale. Insignificant does not even begin to describe what your kind is to me. To the cosmos."

I began to wonder why I was taking all this so *calmly*. Here I was, sitting next to this thing that had caused so much chaos and death, sharing lemonade. For some reason it had taken the form of my grandmother, and it was throwing philosophy at me like some first year grad student.

"You have many questions that you wish to have answered, but I will pick one. Yes. I can replicate what caused your condition. I can make more of you. I will never go hungry, or bored, again."

I was staring at the door to the elevator again, watching it close, but this time it wasn't my own face behind the doors. Randall and a strange woman stared back. I couldn't read her emotions from the look on her face, but Randall regarded me with utter disdain. Before I could act, the doors shut, and the elevator began to rise.

Disgusted that I'd let them get away, I turned back to Timothy, hoping for the best. The pool of blood around him had grown a considerable amount, and his skin was cold when I turned him over. The slash across his neck told me he had been dead before he even hit the ground.

The sound of approaching footsteps forced me to look up. Victoria entered the room, and she did not seem surprised to find me hunched over the corpse of the man we had just met.

"Was it...?"

"Randall? Yes. And what I am guessing is his daughter-in-law."

"I know you said to wait, but I found something."

"What kind of something?"

Victoria shrugged. "I honestly don't know, so I don't even know if it's important. I was coming to get Timothy, but..." Her voice trailed off and she glanced down, not so much at him as at the pool of blood he had left behind.

"Well, show me. Maybe I can make sense of it."

We moved back to the office, and Victoria led me to the computer. The lights had been turned on, and I could more clearly see that the room was drab, even by office standards. There were no decorations; not even a fake plant in the corner. Victoria crossed to the desk and beckoned me to follow. As I came up beside her, she turned the monitor slightly so I could see it better.

There, in what I could only describe as a DOS-style prompt, was a statement, a series of numbers, and a blinking cursor:

```
ENTER COORDINATES:
00.1145.00.00.88756.01
```

"Does this mean what I think it does?" It was difficult to hide the growing excitement in my voice. Surprisingly, *her* mood hadn't changed much at all.

"I think it does. That's why I wanted to talk to Timothy."

"We can go home! We can finally get the fuck out of here!"

"We don't even know where home *is*, remember? Timothy said they had no home beacon, or whatever. We don't know what numbers to put in, or even how many. It may as well be in some other language."

Her statement instantly soured things. She was right, and a small part of myself hated her for being so frank about it, hated that I didn't get more than a taste of that hope. I felt ashamed for hating her, even for an instant. There was no reason to hate her just because she was right.

"Shit. So we're right back where we started."

"Yeah."

A heavy silence settled between us, and I let my eyes wander around the room. There were dozens of binders on the shelves, and I made my way over to some at random. Many were just textbooks, technical things that were far above my level of understanding. However, there was one especially thick binder that caught my eye. On the side was a label sticker, with the phrase 'Beacon Positioning' printed on it in small, dot matrix letters. I picked it up, and carried it back to the desk.

Victoria said nothing as I flipped through the first few pages. They were full of tech-speak; like a glossary of terms and jargon that were way too advanced for me to understand. I was just about to give up and put the binder away again, when the information changed. Each subsequent page was headed by a seventeen digit number divided into groups of two, four, and five numbers. The first one in the log book was unassuming enough:

`00.0000.00.00.00000.00`

Underneath that were the words 'Initial Start Position.' *Hmm.* Something was starting to click, so I flipped through the pages. Each number increased by a single digit, and underneath were descriptions of any findings or events from the excursion. Then, after twelve pages, the numbers changed drastically. They went from all zeroes and a 12 as the last two digits, to this:

`87.5582.12.45.28990.63`

There was no explanation in-between. Apparently the scientists had gotten bored of doing things methodically and by the book.

The first crazy number was described as 'non-existent', which seemed odd to me. There were a few more after that with the same notation, and then several more pages with notes from excursions, like the first pages had. These mission findings were far more interesting than the earlier ones though.

I started reading through some of the notes, hoping to find something that would help us. There was no mention of the place we found ourselves in now, but I noticed that all of the numbers that had actually *led* somewhere had one thing in common: the set of four numbers were always `0000`. What could it mean?

I looked at the computer monitor again, with the numbers `1145` and it hit me like a ton of bricks.

"I don't think the home beacon has a full array of coordinates on its own...It has to be *part* of the coordinate array."

"I don't follow."

I paused, trying to think of a way to explain it. Truth was, I didn't fully grasp it myself. "I think the four digits in the coordinate array set the start. So if we change those, we go nowhere. They *need* to remain constant, depending on where we are."

"And without knowing our own dimension in relation to where we are now..." She sighed deeply. "We have no idea how to work the equipment without Tim. We'll never find the numbers we need. We're fucked."

Our salvation was close enough to touch, but forever out of reach. It was maddening. "Maybe. I dunno."

She pointed at the monitor. "Well...this number is already entered. Do we want to try it?"

I stepped in front of the keyboard but my finger froze over the enter key. Victoria seemed eager to try it out, and part of me figured we had nothing left to lose. But I still couldn't bring my finger down. Someone, most likely Randall, had left this specific number on the screen for a reason. Was it a trap? Were they trying to trick us?

I didn't have time to ponder it further though;. Victoria reached over and hit the enter key for me. I heard a familiar sound coming from the room in the hall and we both went to investigate. A fracture had opened inside, and it looked like a perfectly normal concourse in the mall. But if it was...why had Randall and the woman gone back up in the elevator?

"Mother fucker." Victoria's statement caught me by surprise, and I couldn't hide the grin on my face. She saw it, and managed a half-grin back.

"So, do we try and go through numbers to discover home, or go after Randall and his daughter-in-law?"

I had to think for a minute before I answered. "They need to pay. Plus, they might have the coordinates we need."

She nodded. "I agree. If we had to sit here and try numbers...I'd go mad. I once had to try and unlock a combination lock that I had forgotten the number for. It used five digits...took me about an hour and a half, but I got it."

"What was the number?"

"9-3-7-9-1. And I started with 0-0-0-0-1."

I let out a low whistle. "Well, if we *do* have to try numbers at random, I vote you sit that one out."

She gave me a playful slap on the arm, and I think the banter actually made us feel normal for a few minutes. We moved out of the room and back to the main office.

"Alright. Let's go see if we can pay the good doctor a visit."

"Do you think that beast guy is still up there, waiting for us?"

"I don't think so. I mean, Randall and that other woman got down here easily enough, and they just took the elevator back up."

"How *did* they get down here? There's no way they were here before us, and we didn't see anybody get off the elevator before we bumped into Timothy."

I was about to tell her that I had no more idea than she did when a deep, powerful scream came from the side room, scaring both of us half to death. It sounded exactly like the-

The Minotaur came into view, stomping into the hallway. It looked right, towards the main area, and I prayed it wouldn't notice us inside the office. Victoria and I remained as quiet as we could; I don't think I was even breathing. It started to move towards the main room, and I still didn't move. I didn't move again until it was completely out of sight.

If the Minotaur had gotten in, maybe the fracture was still open. Maybe we could trap it down here. I looked at Victoria, pointed to the side room, and mouthed *follow me*. She nodded to show that she understood, and we moved, ever so quietly, towards the door. The Minotaur was out of sight, but I could hear it thrashing around in the main area. We both crept into the hallway, and were about to enter the side room when the Minotaur stepped into view and saw us. It grunted and started to run.

I grabbed Victoria's wrist and ran for the fracture, which was, thankfully, still open.

"What if it's poison again?!"

"Then at least *that* thing isn't killing us!"

I jumped through, landing near the mall entrance where this whole ordeal had begun. I slammed into Victoria's sales display, sending miniature remote controlled vehicles flying in every direction. I still was holding onto Victoria's hand, and the Minotaur was right behind us.

I felt something pull on her, and turned to look back. Instead of a fracture leading back to the the equipment room, there was just a hazy spot in the air, like ripples on a pond. One of the Minotaur's arms stuck out, gripping Victoria's ankle, tugging hard. I watched in horror as she started to inch back towards the fracture.

Quickly I wrapped my arms around her waist and pulled back as hard as I could, thinking I might be able to wrestle her from its grip. The Minotaur refused to release her, and she began to move back towards the fracture.

"Don't...Don't let it get me!" she yelled. I kept trying to work against the Minotaur's force. No matter how hard I tried, she was slowly getting pulled away from me, closer to the invisible gap between dimensions. Just as her toes were about to pass the threshold, the ripples stopped.

The resistance disappeared with the ripples, and we both fell backwards onto the floor. Victoria shrieked, and I looked to see a hand still wrapped around her ankle. It was cleanly severed at the wrist, blood dripping from the wound.

I quickly reached forward and pried the hand from her ankle. An uneasy sense of déjà vu overcame me as I held, well, my *own* hand and tossed it as far away as I could. Victoria clung to me as we got our bearings and looked around.

I knew that there was no way to be certain, but I thought that this was actually *the* mall. I stood, helping Victoria to her feet. She rubbed at her ankle, but said nothing. I looked one way, and then the next, feeling lost and helpless. We were out of the underground area, but what now? I was clueless.

The setting changed again, and there was my grandmother. I closed my eyes tightly, and took in a deep breath.

"What the fuck do you want now?"

"You will mind your place. I grow tired of your resistance to the inevitable. Come. I have need of you."

"Forget it. I'm not your personal errand boy. And if you're feeling peckish, there's another one of me downstairs."

The thing, in my grandmother's visage, glared at me silently for a long moment, then its lips spread into a smile. It was so warm and inviting, I almost forgot what the thing truly was. Almost.

"Already you entertain me. Good! If only the woman could be made as you are. Oh, the fun we all could have. Ah, well. I suppose we shall simply have to enjoy her until first her body, and then her mind, break."

"Leave her out of this!" I screamed in defiance.

It was already gone, and Victoria was gripping my arm tightly. 'What the hell was that about? Those things will hear us!"

I shook my head and we headed off to a dress store, ducking inside just in case. The lights were off, and we were able to hide towards the back. Sure enough, two of the Shushers came shambling past, trying to find us. Only now I knew they weren't autonomous creatures, they were extensions of that...thing. It had its tendrils deep, and they were only digging deeper now that we had revived it.

"Look," I whispered, "I have no idea how long I can keep resisting that thing. It's in my head, and now it can apparently make me see things whenever it wants. It says it needs me, *wants* me. You...it says that you're expendable."

She took the statement better than I hoped, and just responded, "I see. Well, we need to find a way out of here before it gets rid of me then, don't we?"

I nodded in agreement, but we were practically back at square one. The only way we knew of to access the fractures was back in the facility, and the Minotaur was still trapped down there. And even if we *could* get back there without it killing us, finding the right coordinates to get home would be next to impossible. The odds were stacked against us.

"Randall opened that fracture from somewhere else in the mall, right? We need to find him and force him to open one for us. One to get us back home."

I was making an educated guess, but a man like Randall had to have a foolproof escape plan. You don't just thrust yourself into the most dangerous situation imaginable without a backdoor. Even Houdini kept a key on his person. At least I think he did.

Satisfied that the coast was clear, we crept out of the dress shop, but not before Victoria took a moment to admire one of the dresses.

"If we make it, I'll buy you a whole goddamn shop's worth."

She smirked, dry and humorless. "I have a boyfriend."

My statement hadn't been intended to come across as anything remotely sexual or romantic, so I raised an eyebrow at her, and she smiled, wide. Genuine mirth. If we weren't try-

All Sales Final

ing so hard to be quiet, I would have laughed long and hard at the joke.

The coast was clear. We needed to find Randall, but I had no idea where to look. The only 'secret' installation was the underground facility. Was there a second one somewhere that no one knew about?

The more I thought about it, the less sense that made. Maybe something outside was linked with the fractures? Like that cube? Honestly, trying to figure out *how* he was doing all this was the least of my worries. We needed to find him before we did anything else. Then I could grill him about the smoke and mirrors.

"This way."

I moved in the direction the Shushers had come from. While I knew they were ultimately controlled by the tentacle creature, I had a feeling in my gut that Randall wouldn't be far behind.

We were just about to round a corner when I heard voices. Male and female, arguing.

"-don't care! Either we end this, or we get the fuck out of here!"

"We're too close! We need to finish what we started."

It was Randall, and the strange woman he'd been arguing with before. I recognized the voice. How fortunate that we would run into them now. Probably too fortunate. A small part of me wondered if this was some trick of the creature, to get me to let my guard down. Whatever. I was at the end of my rope. Hell, I had been for quite some time. I threw caution to the wind and stepped out into the open.

"Where's the fucking exit, Randall?"

Both of them spun to face me, their faces full of surprise. They had clearly not expected us to escape.

"You!" Randall rushed towards me and I adopted a defensive stance, ready to come to blows. He stopped short though, jabbing a finger in my direction and the smirk on his face caused my stomach to bottom out. Something was off, wrong.

"I should be thanking you. Because of what you've done, and what you are, you've empowered the creature. Things are falling into place much sooner than anticipated. Perhaps *too* fast..." His voice trailed off and he seemed to be pondering something only he could understand. Then he shook his head, and continued. "It's infatuated with you. I can feel it, right at the edges of my consciousness, but its focus is almost entirely on you. How does that feel? To be in the gaze of a *god*?"

Fuck this. I grabbed him by his shoulders and shook him, hard. "How do we open a fracture to get back home? To our reality?"

Randall shrugged out of my grip, and straightened his shirt before turning his back on me and walked towards the woman. I was fuming, but something kept me from rushing him and tackling him to the ground. Kept me from smashing my fists into his face.

"Randall, this is getting to be too much. You said we could bring Reggie back, but we haven't even *seen* the other him. When does this all get fixed?

"Gina, you know I love you like a daughter, but none of this can happen the way it's supposed to if you're here." Randall lifted his pant leg and pulled a knife from a sheathe clasped to his leg.

"*What?*"

No one had any time to react, especially Gina. Still kneeling, he stabbed upwards, into her midsection, then tore the knife away. Blood and viscera splashed onto the floor as she screamed.

"I TRUS-TRUSTED YOU! WH-WHY?!"

She fell to her knees, feebly scrabbling at the fallen intestines, trying futilely to stuff them back into the wound. Randall callously wiped the blade of the knife against her shoulder as she sobbed and blubbered.

"You knew this was part of it. Or, at least you should have suspected it." He leaned forward and whispered something into her ear that I couldn't hear.

Gina went pale, and fell forward, her head making a sickening crack as it bounced off the tile floor. She was dead.

"She was your son's wife!" I roared at him, aghast at the crime I had just witnessed. I could sense Victoria hovering behind me.

Randall scoffed. "She will be back. It is crucial that I am the only one to experience what comes next."

"What comes next?" Victoria's words were full of dread, fear. If he was willing to kill so coldly to achieve his goals, there was no telling what else he was capable of, no telling what he ultimately wanted.

"Oh, if only you could see what I have seen. Tasted from the chalice of the infinite cosmos..."

"Make some sense, goddammit! Why did you do this?!"

"As I said, It must only be *me*. Then I can bring back everything."

I'd had enough from this madman. At least the creature was clear about its intentions. It wanted to use and abuse me for its own sadistic ends, but at least it was honest about it. Randall...Randall was just going insane. Maybe he'd been insane even before all this started. I stepped forward and caught him across the jaw with a right hook. It made my hand hurt like hell, but it was very satisfying.

He landed on his ass, dropping the knife, and when he looked up at me, his eyes were smoldering with rage. Spitting out blood, he hissed at me, "You are a *fool*. You revived the means of your own torment! You rush towards your destiny like a pig on the track to slaughter. You will *never* escape. Either of you."

He leered at Victoria, and my knee-jerk reaction was to kick him in the stomach. He doubled over, but instead of crying out in pain, he laughed. Just a low chuckle at first, then growing to a howling belly laugh. I started to get nervous, wondering if all this noise was going to attract unwanted attention.

I must have jinxed myself with that thought, but it wasn't Shushers. Instead it was a huge amount of black sludge. I had been wondering if we'd ever see it again. Maybe the creature had sent it now, but that didn't matter. We had to get out of there.

Reaching down, I grabbed Randall's collar and pulled him roughly to his feet, shoving him towards Victoria. Then I picked up the knife and took a good look at it. It wasn't a regular knife; it looked ornamental. Red and blue gemstones were inlaid along the golden hilt, and the blade looked as if it might be silver. I carefully slid it through one of my belt loops and turned back to Randall.

"You're going to show us how to get back home, or I'm going to do to you what you did to Gina."

"You really don't get it, do you?"

"I get that you're some sort of psychopath who brought an entire mall to this hell."

"My god, you really are a simpleton. But that's *wonderful*! That will make it so much easier to manipulate you, to work with the creature to entrap your mind."

"Shut up, Randall. The next words you speak better be about how to get home."

I gave him a shove as we headed towards the main security office. Hopefully we'd be safer in there than we were out here in the open. If the cameras were still working we could at least keep an eye on where the Shushers were, and maybe being able to monitor the mall would help us formulate a way out of here.

I'd beat the information out of him if I had to.

"Ha! This was never about going back. *Only forward*!"

"What the hell are you talking about?"

"There *is* no way back! This was a one-way trip!"

XXI

I pushed the man, hard, and watched him fall into a heap at my feet. He started laughing again, which only made me angrier. I was about to give him a swift kick when Victoria grabbed my arm to get my attention. I didn't kick him, but I didn't take my eyes off of him either.

"This won't solve anything."

Begrudgingly, I had to agree with her. I grabbed Randall and hoisted him back to his feet, giving him a shove to get him going again. I was pretty sure I remembered the way to the security office. I just hoped that the door would actually be unlocked.

"This *mall* was always intended for this *purpose*. Understand? It isn't a fluke that it still has power. It's by design."

"Shut. Up."

He continued, despite my command. "You can't stop it. Your fate is written in *stone*. I, however, have a great destiny that only I may fulfill."

His endless prattling was beginning to get on my nerves. "One more word and I'll knock you out and leave you here for the sludge to find."

"Suit yourself. Let those burning questions continue to smolder. You'll be begging me to talk soon enough."

The rest of the trip was silent, and thankfully we didn't encounter anything we couldn't handle. There was a close brush with three Shushers, but even Randall had the sense to remain silent, and they passed by without so much as glancing in our direction.

When we got to the Security office, I tried the handle. Locked.

"Shit." I tried it again, hoping that maybe it had just been stuck, but to no avail. I turned to Victoria. "We need to search him."

Randall offered no resistance, standing silently as I awkwardly stuffed my hands into his pockets. There was a set of keys in his left front pocket, and I tried each one until I found the one that unlocked the door. We all moved inside, and I closed and locked it behind us. We didn't need any other surprises showing up.

I had no idea how the security system worked. I didn't even know if the cameras were stationary or not. But the monitors were still on, and I crossed the room towards them, scanning the images for any signs of Shushers or ooze. I saw the three Shushers that we'd passed standing around a fountain, eerily still. I squinted a little, and looked closer, but it still took me a minute to realize that the fountain wasn't filled with water, it was filled with ooze.

For a second, I wondered what the purpose of the ooze actually was. The bodies, the Shushers, were controlled by the thing, but the ooze? I wondered if it was some kind of cleanup crew; the antibodies of Purgatory.

"Alright, Randall. You said we'd be begging you to talk, so talk: what the *fuck* do you mean there's no way home?"

He smirked at me, and I really wanted to punch him again. His jaw was already swollen and bruised, though. I didn't know if I'd broken anything last time, but I didn't want to take the chance that a second hit would silence him by accident.

"I meant exactly what I said. This whole excursion was meant to be the end."

"The end of what?" Victoria asked.

"Oh, my dear, I can't tell you *that* yet. There's a certain order in which these events need to proceed."

I walked forward and slugged him in the abdomen, causing him to double over, coughing. It wasn't his smug face, but it still felt good to hit him. I grabbed him by the hair and yanked his head up so we were face to face. "If we're really trapped here, asshole, the first thing I'm going to do is choke the life from your worthless body. Then all the cryptic doubles-peak in the world won't fucking matter. Start talking straight, or you're dead."

Even as the words left my mouth, I felt a chill run down my spine. He was behind everything, but could I really kill him in cold blood like that? I'd never killed anyone before.

"Do you really have the stones, David? Can you do what mus-"

He cried out in pain as the point of a knife suddenly protruded from his shoulder. As it disappeared again, I glanced past him to see Victoria standing there, the strange sil-ver knife in her hands. She had somehow gotten it free of my belt loop without my noticing.

"Tell us everything. Or the next time I slit your throat."

There was no denying the relief I felt that she was will-ing to do this. I doubted that I actually had the resolve to do anything worse than throw a few punches.

"You...you can't!" Randall hissed out from between clenched teeth.

She moved quickly, stabbing through his other shoul-der before either he or I had a chance to react. He fell to his knees as she pulled the blade out, the front of his shirt soaked with blood. There was a sheen of sweat on his skin now, and for the first time I saw true fear on his face. He hadn't expected this behavior from Victoria. She was the wrench in his ma-chine.

"I can. And I will." She advanced on him menacingly. "Grab his arm."

I complied, wondering what she was up to.

Randall resisted feebly. "Please...not with that...blade..." His breathing was ragged.

Victoria grabbed onto his hand, slammed it up against the wall, and held the blade against his index finger.

"Talk. Now."

Her face was blank, but her eyes burned with hatred. I knew, without a doubt, that she would kill him without hesita-tion if he didn't give us the information she wanted.

"Very well, I'll talk. *Bitch*."

She brought the knife down, and I heard a sickening crunch as it cut through the finger, severing tendons and grinding against the bone. The finger dropped with a plop on the floor, and Randall wailed.

When he stopped blubbering, Victoria moved the knife to the next finger in line.

"I would suggest being a bit more polite," I advised. He had stopped struggling, so I let go of his arm and got down on my haunches to look him in the face. He was sweating more now, eyes half-lidded. I wondered if he was going into shock. I gently slapped his face.

"Stay with us. We're not done yet. What was the purpose of all this?"

"Teleportation is so mundane; the stuff of science fiction. Moving atoms a mere ten yards was *inadequate*. Using the fractures we could traverse immeasurably greater distances *without* the teleportation process, and using only a fraction of the energy."

"The creature was actually quite easy to capture when we discovered it. It had never encountered anything like *living* humans before, and, naturally, it was curious. Its unique brainwaves and energy were what enabled us to traverse not only distance, but dimensions as well."

"We know all this. Timothy explained it, but he didn't tell us about the creature."

Randall coughed and smirked, shaking his head. "He knew very little. The project changed after that point. *I* changed. It was something I discovered late one night, and it put everything into perspective. The creature helped."

"Discovered what?" Victoria was standing next to me now, still holding the knife. Randall tucked in his injured hand and cradled it against his chest.

"The ultimate gateway. Absolute, irrefutable proof of *heaven*. But, of course, we were unable to cross over. That was when I turned to ritual and the supernatural. That was where the creature truly shined. It gave me ideas. Symbols. Pieces to the whole. It, you see, had *come* from that wonderful place."

"You *killed* because the thing told you to? So you could enter some damn, fairy tale fracture?!"

The smirk melted from his face and turned into a sneer. "Don't you *dare* judge me. If you had seen the wonderful things I have...heard the same promises and tantalizing whispers...you, too, would do whatever was necessary. Besides, they wait for me."

"They're dead. They're not waiting anywhere."

"The faith of a mustard seed, David. You only need faith the size of a mustard seed to move a mountain."

He started to stand on shaking limbs. We let him, but I was wary; even heavily injured there was no telling how dangerous he was.

"How do we get out of here?"

"I told you. It was a one-way trip."

"I don't believe you." Victoria moved forward again and held the knife to his throat, resting the blade against his flesh.

"Okay! I'll...I'll tell you."

She relaxed slightly, but kept the blade at the ready, close to his throat.

"The only way out, is to move forward. I have done everything expected of me. I have proven myself. Have you, *whore*?"

"I swear to god, Randall, this is your last chance. If you don't talk, I *will* kill you."

"God? *God?!* Neither of you have been listening to a word I've been saying, have you?" He glared at me. "*I will **become** god!*"

Victoria took a step back, a look of profound shock on her face. But it only lasted a moment before being replaced by hysterical laughter that left her doubled over.

"You've lost it. You're even crazier than me!"

"Perhaps. But mine is the kingdom."

He caught us by surprise, lunging forward and grabbing the knife by the blade, pulling it out of Victoria's hand. Then he held the tip of the blade to his own throat, glaring at us with a wild look in his eyes.

"You want answers to questions you didn't even know to ask. But you can't handle the answers for the few feeble-minded questions you do manage to stammer out. Everything changes, and it is by *my* hand! And mine alone!"

He began to press the blade harder against his skin, and I saw a drop of fresh blood appear. "Randall, take it easy. Maybe Victoria went a little overboard, but can you really blame her? *Us?* We just want a way home."

"I am on my way to *heaven*."

Still holding the blade on himself, he crossed to the monitors and glanced down at the keyboard. Neither Victoria or I moved, afraid of what he might do if we got too close. He made a few keystrokes and the monitors began to shut down, one by one. When then came back on, each screen had a command prompt that looked exactly like the one in the lab. *This* was the backup site. No wonder he had been able to keep track of us.

"Okay, Randall…" I said, trying to get his attention back on me. "You can do whatever it is that you came here to do. We just want to get home. Send us back, and we'll call it even."

"David, you can't be-"

I shot Victoria a pleading look, and, thankfully, she didn't protest any further. All the death and destruction we'd witnessed…It wasn't something that *anyone* could forgive or forget, but I was far more concerned with getting out of this hell.

I looked back at Randall, who met my gaze with a smirk. He'd already entered a set of coordinates into the computer.

"It's time to move forward, David. Perhaps I will take pity on you and deliver you from this torment. All I ask is your eternal worship."

"Randall, please!"

Continuing to smirk, he simply stated, "And he went forth conquering, and to conquer."

He hit enter.

The sound of a fracture surrounded us, but I couldn't see one opening. Randall used his blood-soaked hand and drew three symbols on the wall, slapping his open palm against it. The wall fell away and in its place was a brilliant light. It should have been blinding, but I could look directly into it without flinching. It was terrifying and welcoming. Cold and warm. Beginnings and Endings. All things, all choices. All mistakes and all triumphs. It overwhelmed me and I wept in pure joy.

In that moment Randall thrust the knife into his own neck.

"NO!" I screamed, reaching for him. But his body was already falling forward, into the brilliant light. By the time I reached the place he had been standing, it had swallowed him up. As quickly as it had begun, it was over.

I fell to my knees, keenly aware of an absence in my mind, my body, in my very *soul*, caused by the light's disappearance. After a silent moment, I turned to Victoria.

"What...what was that?"

There was no reply. Victoria was gone.

XXII

I sat there, unable to move, or even to think. Victoria had been there one moment, and was gone the next. Had she somehow gone through the portal without Randall or me noticing? Or had she run as soon as she had the chance?

For ten, maybe fifteen seconds, I found I honestly didn't care. I still longed for whatever had been on the other side of the portal that Randall opened. When reality came crashing back on me and I realized that I was truly alone, I started to panic. I didn't want to be the only one left in this damned place, with no way to get back home. At least with Victoria around, I had someone to talk to.

I opened the door of the security office and peeked out. There was no sign of her, but I didn't dare call out, for fear of attracting unwanted attention. I couldn't explain it; in my mind there was no way she could have gone through the portal or left the room without my noticing.

I shut the door slowly, and turned back to the monitors. There was a man standing there, and I jumped when I saw him. I was sure I'd never seen him before, but he was just so utterly average that I forgot him almost as soon as I took my eyes off him. He wasn't normal, but I felt positive that he wasn't a manifestation of the creature.

"David. I'd offer to shake your hand, but I have a thing about...*germs*."

The way he hesitated before he said the word germs, gave me the distinct feeling that he wasn't talking about what might be covering my hand, but about me as a whole. It was unnerving.

"Where's Victoria?"

His eyebrows raised and he tilted his head to the side."Interesting. Usually I'm bombarded with so many questions that don't really need answers, but you go right to the heart of the matter. I appreciate how blunt you are."

Then, nothing. I expected him to continue, to answer my question, but neither of us said a word until I repeated myself. "Where is Vict-"

"I will never understand my need for any of this. These...petri dishes, overflowing with muck and decay and filth. Failed experiments, all. And yet I continue. As one fails, I build three more."

"What are you talking about? I just want to know what happened to Victoria." I tried to look him in the eye, and started to forget all my questions. He shot me an icy glare, as if I had just insulted his mother. Pain bloomed behind my eyes.

"Stubborn. I'd forgotten that." As he spoke I quickly turned away as the pain grew too intense, and his face faded from my mind. Even though I tried as hard as possible, I couldn't recall more than a hazy outline. What was this? "Listen, David. You might think my being here is part of some plan or divine providence. It's not."

"How do you know me?"

"I know all of them." He sighed. "Unfortunately."

"All the...me?" I asked, wondering if he meant my copies.

He barked out a dismissive laugh. "No. At any rate, you will never comprehend what I want, or why I'm here. So why bother?"

"Because a strange man has shown up out of nowhere, right after a friend of mine disappeared. Right after that..."

The portal. The light. The man before me.

"Was...was that heaven? Are you god?" I asked, hardly believing the words as they came out of my mouth, barely more than a whisper.

"You're reaching. Stop it. There is no Deus ex machina for you, or anyone else here, for that matter. Not because I can't. *I won't.* The answer to both of your simple, stupid questions is no."

He was being belligerent, talking down to me like I was a child. Yet, I found I could not muster the words to speak my mind, nor to talk back. I was in a sort of trance as I looked off to the side, continuing to listen as he spoke at me, rather than to me.

"Randall messed with the order. I am putting things back. Or, I would be, if he hadn't fucked with it so badly in the first place."

"Is he god now?"

"No one is god. They *all* are gods. It's like the town whore. *Everyone expects to get a turn.* Now shut up."

He walked past me and swung the door open, walking out into the mall. Compelled, I followed him. He seemed determined to find something, but I had no idea what he could possibly be searching for.

"Come on out, you little fuck! I know you're up and about again!" The words bellowed from his unassuming frame with a force that caused me to cower slightly.

A moment later, my grandmother appeared, sneering at the man. In a blink she transformed back to the creature's natural form. The mass of writhing tentacles and the sharp, jagged beak sticking out of the the middle of its eye.

"You have no business being here, First."

"You are correct. And normally, I wouldn't think of dirtying myself. But *you* let this happen."

"Impossible. They are all dead, save my special *treat*."

"A woman yet lives, your treat is insufferable, and Randall completed the ritual. You failed. Know what that means?"

"You must be joking. Does He know of this?"

"I wouldn't be surprised if it was all His idea."

"Agreed."

They continued their conversation, but I was having trouble understanding it all. There was still something about the whole situation that didn't make sense. I looked at the creature and started to feel the same pain I felt whenever I tried to look at the man.

"David."

The man called for my attention, and I answered without looking. "What? Am I going to get some answers?"

"I wasn't entirely truthful. That *was* a gate to heaven. Randall performed a ritual to try and overthrow God himself.

He succeeded. I am Lucifer, and this is Baal. We're trying to fix the mistake. Will you help us?"

I just stood there, staring at the floor, processing everything that had happened, and everything he had just said. It was all starting to make sense, now that he had put it into words. The project, the evidence of the rituals, where we were...Randall was trying to reach heaven, and he had succeeded. But there was still a nagging feeling in the pit of my stomach. I focused on an image in my mind, and slowly looked up. There was a hand outstretched before me.

The skin had taken on a reddish tint, and when I looked into his face I saw the stereotypical devil: horns, forked tail, and even the pointed goatee. His lips were curled into a smile and Baal was right behind him, tentacles undulating gently.

I looked past Lucifer and right into the eye-beak. "You fucked up."

I blinked, and was suddenly back in the security room, on the floor. Victoria was leaning over me, shaking my shoulders, apparently trying to wake me up. Randall was nowhere to be seen. Had the thing with the fracture even happened?

Victoria was saying something to me, but all I could hear were the creature's words thundering through my mind. *You are far, far too clever for your own good. You will serve, and I will seal the contract with blood, if necessary.*

"I know your name you piece of shit..." I mumbled as Victoria helped me sit up.

YOU WILL SERVE!

Whether or not the thing's name was actually Baal, at least I had something to call it. I wasn't sure how I knew it had been a trick, but I knew how to test it. I had to fill my mind, flood my thoughts with the most asinine image possible. And it worked.

"Who's name? What are you talking about?"

The voice was gone, but I didn't know for how long. "The creature. I think its name is Baal. It tried to trick me after Randall went through the portal to heaven."

"Heaven?" Victoria looked at me like I had just sprouted a third ear on my forehead.

"The fracture...that portal of brilliant light. He killed himself and fell through. Remember?"

"David...there was no portal of light. Randall didn't kill himself."

"What?? But..I..." Had it all been part of Baal's ruse, his attempt to get me to serve willingly? Did I have to agree, to submit, before it could exploit me?

"You just sat there as he opened the fracture. He said something about the kingdom, and walked through. There was no light. No brilliance. It was just...a void. A black void. You were staring at it, started to cry, and then collapsed.

I couldn't trust my own senses. I didn't know if this was the real Victoria or just part of another illusion. I stood, wobbling slightly as if I were trying to walk for the first time after spending weeks in bed. I was weak, and my muscles ached.

"You need to take a minute to rest."

"No...not yet."

There would be no rest for me, not unless I finished this. I had to test my theory. I turned to face Victoria, balling my hands into fists.

"Where did we first meet?"

"What? David, what are you-"

"It's a simple question. Where did we first meet?" I did everything I could to focus on something, anything else, other than the truth. We met in high school. She was my sister's friend. She was a co-worker. We met at the strip club where she worked part time. Anything and everything, as quickly as I could.

"We met...we...we..." She looked like she was concentrating hard, trying to focus, but couldn't.

I strode over to her, balled my hand into a fist, and swung. When my fist made a solid connection with her face, and sent her sprawling across the floor, I felt sick. I made a mistake. I was wrong. Oh god, what had I done?

"Victoria! I..I am so sorry...I thought you were...that...thing!!"

Groaning out in pain, she turned to me, blood drooling out of her mouth. The corners curled into a smirk as she looked right at me. A hand went to her breast and started to lewdly rub it. "Finally, a real man."

All regret left me. "Enough of your games!! Show me the truth, Baal!!"

I was gasping for breath as I bolted upright. I was in the room, again, with Victoria across from me. I looked around frantically, but there was no evidence of Randall or the fracture.

"What happened?" I turned to Victoria. She was pressed up against the wall, evidence of tears having run down her cheeks.

"Randall fell into the fracture, you reached for him, then your body began to convulse. I tried to stop you, but you weren't...responsive." It was then that I noticed the bruise on her cheek. The sick feeling in the pit of my stomach came back. I must have struck her.

"Victoria, if I hurt you..."

She wiped at her cheeks, being careful of the bruise and shook her head. "You weren't yourself. That isn't why I'm crying, anyway."

"Why, then?"

"The light. Whatever it was. Whatever Randall was attempting...it made me feel so...complete. As soon as it was gone I felt like... like something was missing."

I slowly nodded, knowing exactly how she felt.

"The creature...I call it Baal now. It's trying more and more desperately to get me to agree to serve it. I still don't know why it doesn't just force me."

She shrugged and stared at the floor. We both sat in silence. I recalled what I had done in Baal's dreamworld so I stood and moved to the monitors. None of what was on the screen made any sense to me, so I hit the enter key one more time, hoping for the best.

Nothing happened. There really was no way out. No magic portal. No gateway to heaven. No salvation. Randall was supposedly on his way to becoming the new messiah, and Victoria and I were here. Left to wallow in our own shit.

In frustration I grabbed the keyboard and slammed it against the desk. Over and over, until keys went flying off with each strike. Finally, it reached its limit and snapped in two, a large chunk of circuit board breaking off and bouncing against the wall where the fracture had been.

Some wishful part of me, perhaps the one little bit that had never grown up, hoped that maybe that would be the magic action to make everything better. I just stared at the piece as it fell, unceremoniously, to the ground, bounced twice, and lay still.

"Hope. Hopelessness. Over and over. Endless. This realm truly is purgatory." My voice sounded weak, hollow, as I spoke the words. I let the rest of the keyboard drop to the ground with a clatter. The monitors blinked back to security camera feeds. I watched them, honestly because I had nothing better to do.

That's when I saw it. At first everything looked exactly as it had when we first entered. Shushers here and there, the black ooze near the fountain...but as I watched I realized there was something moving. With purpose. It was fast, and I couldn't tell it if was another creature or a person. When it finally moved out of range of the cameras, I realized where I had seen it last. I knew that area. *This* area. My eyes grew wide and I turned to Victoria, rushing over to her and helping her up.

"Hurry, we've got to get-"

The door to the security office flung open.

XXIII

The figure burst into the room, knocking me back as it rushed over to the monitors. I could see now that it was a man, his clothing threadbare and tattered, hair long and greasy, and he smelled quite unwashed. He cursed loudly as he saw the ruins of the keyboard.

"Fuck! I'm too late."

Even though it was hoarse, I recognized the voice, and my blood ran cold. Victoria looked from me to the man, and then back again, her eyes going wide. She recognized it as well. The ruined man standing before us was...Randall.

"What the fuck is going on? What did you do?!" I rushed at him, grabbing him by the shoulders and pushing him up against the wall, using my arm to put pressure on his neck as I held him in place. Surprisingly, he offered no resistance. The look in his eyes wasn't that of the insane, confident man who had opened a portal, but one who was broken and defeated.

I held him as long as I could, but the smell wafting from him was enough to make my eyes water, even though I did my best to breath through my mouth. I could *taste* how bad he smelled. I gagged slightly and let go, coughing as he just stood there, staring at the floor, mumbling the same thing over and over.

"Too late. Too late. Always too late."

Victoria took a hesitant step towards him and asked, "Too late for what?"

"To stop myself! To end this circle of hell!" He screamed and slammed his fists against the wall, before repeating himself and crumpling to the floor. Randall began to blubber and cry. Whatever had happened to him after he went through that portal, this was not the same man as before.

"Randall...you need to tell us what happened."

"No. Not myself. Himself. Our self." He shut his eyes tightly, as if to try and focus past some sort of intense pain. He began to run his fingers through his filthy hair, tugging at it roughly. More than a few strands came loose.

"He's lost it." Victoria looked at me, and I was afraid she would see the look on my face. The look that betrayed that this could be my fate as well. The self-realization that this shell of a man on the floor could very well be me, if Baal got its way. I quickly turned away.

"Lost it or not, he has answers that we need." Doing my best to ignore the smell, I got down on my haunches and tried to reason with him. "Randall. Think. Why are you too late? What have you come to do?""

"It's not a river. It's a goddamn wheel. Ouroboros forever and ever. I keep doing the wrong things. I keep failing. Have to get it right. Have to. Have to."

He stood and headed towards the door. Victoria stood in his way, holding her hands up in an attempt to stop him.

"Please, you need to just take it easy for a mome-"

He shoved her aside so hard she stumbled and fell. "No time! The wheels turns! I must try again!"

I moved over to help Victoria back to her feet. "Are you alright?"

She nodded. "Yes. But he isn't making sense. Wheel? Ouro...Orawb...what did he say?"

"Ouroboros." I tried to recall what the term meant. I knew I had heard it before, but I was having difficulty grasping it from my memories. It was almost as if every time I got near to the answer, it was moved further away. Were I a more paranoid man, I would blame Baal for what was going on.

Finally, it came to me. "It's a snake that eats itself or something...forever stuck in a loop of life and death. I think."

"But why would Randall be talking about it?"

I watched him leave the room, and started to follow. "I think I'm starting to understand. Remember what Timothy said about the way time moves here?"

"Different for everyone."

"It explains why he," I motioned to Randall, "looks like a goddamn hermit. But what if time was also on a loop?"

"David. Just stop. Everything about this place gives me a headache, and it seems to grow more and more convoluted with each passing step."

"Maybe. But it seems to be the only explanation. Maybe that's why Baal is so set on me giving myself to it. So it can live in the cycle forever?"

I was grasping. Even as I spoke the words, they seemed far-fetched, and more science fiction than fact. I also couldn't shake the feeling that there was something I was forgetting about the Ouroboros, or that I was recalling it incorrectly.

Out in the open, it was hard not to feel exposed. Thankfully Randall kept quiet as we walked, and either didn't know or didn't care that we were following him. I wanted to continue questioning him, but didn't want to risk drawing unnecessary attention.

I hadn't realized it, but we were heading into a section of the mall that I didn't recognize. It was mostly electronics and specialty stores; nothing out of the ordinary. Randall turned and entered a model hobbyist store, and headed for the counter. Victoria and I followed, but as soon as we walked in we were hit with a foul smell.

"What...what *is* that?" She asked as she held her hand over her face.

I had a guess, so I moved forward and towards the counter. There, on the ground, was a dead body. It was so badly decomposed, with the clothing in tatters, that it was impossible to tell who it had been. I turned towards Victoria and shook my head, holding out a hand to keep her back. There was no need for her to see this.

"Why did you bring us here, Randall? What did you want us to see?"

"Wheel. Circle. Circle...starts again. New time. *Old* time. All the same."

He was mumbling, and I was done playing games. "Answer me, goddammit. What were you trying to stop and what is going on here? Who is that?" I pointed at the corpse.

"Myself. You. Us. Them. Can't be sure. Won't ever be sure until I stop it. Stop him."

It was hopeless. "Come on, we need to leave." I spoke to Victoria as I turned to go. "This is getting us nowhere."

"Nowhere is exactly where we need to be."

As Randall spoke, the room seemed to shift slightly. At first it was barely noticeable, then it felt as though it were spinning wildly, even though I knew I was standing still. It was beginning to give me a headache so I shut my eyes. I heard Victoria groan in discomfort, so at least I knew I wasn't alone in this. When a few moments of silence had passed, I finally dared to look and found that the room was stationary once more..

Randall was still there, but the smell of the body was gone. Instead, all I could detect was the faintest odor of copper. I glanced down, and the body was there, but it was no longer decomposed.

It was no one I recognized, but I could tell they had been dead for several hours. There were several stab wounds in the torso, and a large pool of blood surrounded them.

"Did...did we go *back* in time??" I looked at Randall, who seemed to be looking right through me. He shrugged, and then it hit me. The Ouroboros, the snake, it didn't mean a circle. It represented *infinity*. This place was infinite in its possibilities. And either Randall had discovered a spot where the flow was disrupted, or going through the portal had given him that ability.

"Too far. Too far. Need to wait."

"What do you mean? Did we go back too much?" I started to get hopeful. If we had gone back far enough, perhaps we could avoid this entire ordeal. The fact that the body was fresh, and not putrefying, was certainly lending itself to my theory.

"TOO. FAR."

The room began to move again. He seemed focused, obsessed even, with that singular moment when he went into the portal. If Victoria and I could leave the store, we might be able to stay in the past, might be able to get back home.

I felt an overwhelming urge to stay in the shop. Something about it made me feel comfortable, safe. As if nothing going on outside these four walls could hurt me in any way whatsoever. I decided not to trust that feeling. Nothing in this dimension...world...*whatever* it was called, had made me feel safe before. Anything that did...had to be some sort of trap. I grabbed onto Victoria's arm and ran for the door, just as the room began to spin faster.

Moving was slow, every step labored, but we managed to burst through the door and land right in my grandmother's garden. She stood, hands on her hips, foot tapping, as she began to scold us.

"You are starting to become an annoyance, David."

"What? Where...where are we?" Victoria was confused, and I almost forgot that she hadn't been privy to the previous conversations between myself and Baal.

There was genuine shock on its face and in its voice. "She can't be here. I called to you, David."

"She's here now, so deal with it. Wasn't expecting me to break your 'wheel' now, were you?"

The thing in the shape of my grandmother glared at me with pure malice. "Worm. I knew you would flee. I knew you would not. You've done both, and I've allowed both. But in no occurrence have you ever brought *her*."

"So this has happened before?"

Ignoring my question, Baal continued. "Time is my plaything. You think you've outsmarted me with this, but it won't matter in the end. Randall thought he could become as a god. Look at him now. Broken. *You* could have been as close to a god as I am. But instead I will *use* you as sustenance. *All of you.*"

"But you can't unless I agree, isn't that right?"

Her cracked lips curled into a sneer. She didn't reply, but I knew I was right. "You're bound by some cosmic force that forbids you from outright taking what you want, unless it agrees. I've caught your eye and you've tried, who knows how many times, to get me to agree. But each time I've won."

The smug confidence in my voice did little to hide the abject terror I was feeling at that moment. There was no reason, aside from Baal's interest in me, to keep me alive. If I proved too difficult a prize, or didn't play along, it could destroy me in an instant. It was already in my head, playing games.

"Won? No. You're merely advancing towards my side of the board."

We were suddenly back in the field from my first dream. I was a boy again, and felt the same euphoric freedom as I stripped off my clothing and took flight. Again I gouged my eyes from my skull, all to please Baal. My dark god had a name now, and it made me so happy.

So why was I still crying? Why could I still see? Everything was wrong, no matter how much I wanted it to feel right. It was Victoria. She was there with me, screaming as the dream tried to take her as well. Baal's tentacles shot out of the dark sky, wrapping quickly around us both.

I was a man again, regaining my senses as I felt the wriggling flesh constrict against me. I heard Victoria's screams take on a fevered pitch and turned to see what was happening.

Her body was spread-eagle as the tentacles pulled at her limbs. She was stretched out so taut that it seemed she would rip apart at any second.

"No! Don't hurt her!!"

The tension eased for a moment, as Baal's true voice filled my mind. *Then serve. You may have brought a new piece to the board, David. But it will be my linchpin.*

I hesitated, and it ripped her arm off. Blood gushed from the wound as she flailed about, screaming and crying.

"NOOO!!!"

Save her. I will allow it! A single generosity: I will release her. I will spare her this and all future torment, as your reward for giving me the final piece I covet. You. Serve, David.

I watched as she started to go into shock, the color draining from her face. "Promise me. Promise me you'll let her go, you'll send her back. You can, can't you?"

I can.

I thought through my next words carefully. "Promise me you will *restore* her. And that no physical or mental harm will come to her. That you will send her back to where she belongs. That your 'release' isn't death, but her life."

This is why I wanted you, David. Always so clever. In a blink, her arm was back, attached to her body. *Now. Serve.*

This was it. I was trusting some dark deity to hold its end of the bargain. I didn't even know if it really *was* the Baal from my own mythology, but I still used the name as I entered the dark pact. I looked over at Victoria one last time. She was out cold, but I could tell she was breathing.

"Baal, I agree. I will serve. You...you may take me."

Everything went black, and I had the sensation of falling. Then, the most wonderfully horrible experience of pain and pleasure melding into one sensation. I was torn asunder, and my mind opened.

I would serve.

XXIV

"Uncle David!"

My nephew, Xander, came bounding down the walkway towards me before I had even gotten out of my car. I managed to kick the door shut just as he leapt up into my arms. He'd gotten bigger since the last time I saw him.

"Hey, Squirt. Where's your mom?"

"Doing stuff." His reply was helpful. I decided to let him know how helpful by tickling him until he was a squirming, giggling mess.

I gently I let him down onto the lawn and rephrased my question. "Is she in the kitchen getting your cake ready?"

His eyes lit up at the mention of cake and he nodded vigorously. Jumping up he ran back into the house, calling for her. I went to the trunk of my car and pulled out his gift. I had always been a hack when it came to wrapping things, so I had opted to put it into a festive bag, along with some colored tissue paper. Being his favorite uncle, I had also decided to throw a few twenties into the card, just in case he didn't like what I bought him.

Granted, I was his *only* uncle, but I wasn't going to let something like a lack of opposition lull me into a false sense of security. For a moment I wondered if it was too much; the remote controlled helicopter had cost fifty dollars, and there was another sixty in the card. I didn't linger on the notion for too long.

I was sure my sister would tell me if it was too much; she loved to give me an earful about spoiling her child. If she did, I'd just tell her to put the money away for some other time. The kid was seven. What was he going to remember?

A nagging buzz irritated the back of my brain, like a memory trying to assert itself, but I brushed it off and headed inside. It was probably just anticipatory dread of dealing with my sister.

As soon as I walked through the door, I heard her voice from inside the kitchen. "You better take your shoes off, David! You know the rules!"

I frowned. I hated taking my shoes off anywhere other than my own house, but I complied regardless. Sometimes she forgot, and by the time she remembered I'd already been wearing them for so long that she wouldn't bother fighting about it. No such luck today. Kicking them off, I dropped the gift onto the coffee table with the rest and walked into the kitchen.

Xander and two of his friends went running past, barely acknowledging my presence. It was then I noticed those were the only other kids, besides Xander, that I had seen. My sister must have noticed my curiosity, as she addressed it first thing.

"This year I told Xander that we were going to keep things small. I only wanted two or three kids. You remember what happened last year."

Yeah. The kid decided to invite his entire class. "What, you didn't want to play host to twenty-two, barely potty-trained, kids again?" I smirked as she shot me an icy glare.

"What did you get him, anyway?"

I glanced around, making sure he wasn't in earshot. "A remote-controlled helicopter. Thing cost me fifty bucks!"

Susan frowned, her brow furrowing slightly as she turned away from icing the cake. "David, I've told you I don't like how much you spoil Xander."

"Come on, Susie. It's his birthday, for Christ's sake. When was the last time you saw him so happy? I mean, since..."

I let my voice trail off. I hadn't meant to bring it up, and I regretted it as soon as her eyes began to water.

"Jesus, Susan, I'm sorry. I didn't mean-"

"Don't. It's fine. And you're right. Ever since Brandon was killed, it's been...difficult. I just don't want him thinking happiness and joy comes from *things*."

"You've raised him well. There's no way that he'll become *that* spoiled. Trust me."

She smiled a little, and then wiped her eyes with the back of her wrist. "Still, next time go a little smaller, okay?"

I held up my hands, deciding to leave the cash in the envelope a surprise for now. "Alright, next time I will."

"Fifty dollars huh? She musta been cute."

"Who?"

"The woman that suckered you into buying such an expensive toy." Susan laughed at her own joke, and she had a point; I doubt I would have been swayed into the decision I made had the saleswoman not been so attractive. I couldn't recall her name, but I knew I liked her the moment I saw her.

"Will you go get the kids? I want to do cake and presents."

"Sure thing."

I headed out into the living room, the last place I had seen Xander and his friends run off to. Nothing. I headed down the hall to his room and pushed open the door. Inside, there was a dead cow.

The head was missing, and the entrails had all burst from the midsection like some disgusting piñata. The smell was overwhelming, and I turned away, gagging. I began to panic. Why the *fuck* was there a dead cow in Xander's room?!

Turning back, everything was normal. No cow, no smell. Just three little boys making fart noises and laughing hysterically at one another. Xander looked up at me.

"Hello, David. Did something bother you?"

"N-no...Uh...your mom wants to do cake and presents."

"Cake!!" All three yelled in unison as they darted past me and back into the kitchen. I stayed a moment longer, looking over his room. An uneasy feeling settled into the pit of my stomach as I stood there. It had seemed far too real to be a mere hallucination, but what other explanation could there have been?

By the time I headed back to where everyone was, Susan was lighting the candles, and she looked to me to begin singing. I started the Happy Birthday song, and everyone joined in. I then added my favorite 'and many more from channel four' line to the end, which made Xander laugh, just like every year. He blew out the candles, and soon the kids were stuffing their mouths with cake.

"Hey, Susan?" I followed her into the living room, as she arranged the gifts for Xander to open.

"Hm?"

"Did...did you notice anything strange just a moment ago?"

"Strange how? Other than you standing in Xander's doorway like you'd seen a ghost."

"I thought I saw something."

"What?" She looked up at me, expectantly waiting for the answer. I wanted to tell her what I had seen; I never kept anything from my sister, no matter how insane it might have seemed at the time. But for some reason, I couldn't spit it out. She shook her head at me and basically brushed me off.

"Whatever. Go see if the kids are done and bring them here. I want to get gifts out of the way so the boys can continue to play."

I nodded and went to go grab them. But, when I turned the corner to where the dining table was, it was empty. There was no evidence that anyone had even been there in years. Everything looked rundown and dilapidated; there were stains on the ceiling and floor, paint was peeling off the walls, and there was a dark splotch across the sliding glass door. The backyard beyond the glass didn't seem to be in any better shape. It was completely overgrown, and the dark red sky filled me with dread. Blinking hard, I rubbed my eyes and there was Xander, happily munching on cake.

"You okay, Uncle David?"

"Your uncle acts like my blind dog. She just stands there and stares, too. Is he blind?"

Xander looked confused for a moment, then looked at me and asked, "Are you *blind*, Uncle David?"

I was about to answer when he continued. "Blind to that which is right before you? Blind to the truth?"

"Xander, what are yo-"

"Time for presents!" My sister's cheery voice interrupted from behind me, and the kids quickly finished off their cake and ran to go see what the birthday boy got.

Something weird was going on. Maybe I'd eaten something that wasn't agreeing with me. I decided to swear off any food from mall food courts. At least for the foreseeable future.

When I turned around, I saw nothing but pure, unfiltered joy in that kid's face, and anything that was worrying or bothering me seemed to melt away.

By the time he opened my gift, he had gotten a robot and an action figure from his friends, and a set of building blocks from his mother. He opened the card first, and started to scream happily as the twenties fell into his lap. Susan shot me a 'we'll talk later' look but I just shrugged and mouthed 'next time'. She shook her head at me.

Xander greedily stuffed his hand into the bag, and the look of joy immediately turned to confusion, then fear. He ripped his hand out of the bag, and it was covered in blood. Both his mother and I jumped up and rushed over to him. I was concerned that the toy had somehow gotten broken and cut him. Maybe I hadn't realized how sharp the props were.

"Are you alright, honey?! Show mommy!" She grabbed his hand, and began to inspect it. Then her nose wrinkled, and she leaned in to sniff at his hand, recoiling again immediately.

"What the *fuck*?! It smells like death."

I grabbed the bag and upended it, spilling the contents onto the table. Out fell a cat. The cat that I had when I was the same age as Xander. The cat that I saw get hit by a car. The cat that I couldn't bear to let go of, that I had hidden in a box under my bed for weeks before the smell finally alerted my parents.

My dead cat Fester was lying in a decaying heap on my sister's coffee table. Then he turned to me and meowed.

I felt the ground give out under me, and such intense pain that it felt like my skin was being pulled right off my body. I opened my mouth to scream, but no sound came out. Horrible realization flooded my mind as I remembered *exactly* where I was.

I was still in Purgatory, with Baal. And this was yet another of his tricks to destroy my mind.

As far as I knew, he had held up his end of the bargain and sent Victoria back to where she belonged. I had no way of knowing for sure, but the idea that he had was the one thing I clung to. I think it was the only thing keeping me from completely losing what was left of my mind.

How much time had passed? It was impossible to tell. I had been killed, re-killed, reborn, and reworked so many times and gone through so many dark scenarios, like my nephew's birthday, that I had lost count. At least this time the item in the bag wasn't his father's head.

David. I didn't give you permission to stop.

Early on, I discovered that I had a small measure of control in this place. When I realized that it was a 'nightmare' that I was trapped in, I could focus and end it. The pain that followed was nearly unbearable, but I think it was the pain that gave me the clarity to reassert control over the situation. "I didn't give you permission to start." This ability infuriated Baal to no end.

Silence. Sometimes he would engage in the banter, if it pleased him, other times he would just leave me in a state of perpetual darkness, until the next time he had use for me.

You agreed to serve. Serve!

This time was different. When he spoke that single word it reverberated through my mind. I felt like my soul was being shredded, and this time when I opened my mouth to scream the sound came long and hard. I could feel the strain on my face as I gave in to the pain. I couldn't think straight, I couldn't even comprehend what was happening until it was over. Then, a split-second later, it started again.

This was the first time Baal had used pain to discipline me. I could feel him...*chuckle* as I writhed and tried to resist. He threw me again through all the nightmares that I had experienced. The corn field. The visions. The deaths of loved ones, both the real memories and the horrific imaginings that he had forced upon me. There was no hope here, only despair.

There is something I wish to show you, David.

"Please...No..more." The pain wouldn't stop. Why wouldn't it stop?? I was getting frantic, panicked. Was this going to be my new existence?

Yes. But first, you must look upon what I have sown, for you, David. A wonderful gift blooms.

"Wh-what...gift?"

I was back in the mall. It was the first time since my nightmares had begun that he had brought me back to this place. I dared to wonder if it really was the mall or not.

It is. I have no need for illusions. For now.

Baal was fully inside my head, so even my own thoughts betrayed me. There was almost nothing I could hide from him. I probably could have communicated with him strictly through my thoughts, but I didn't want to lose myself like that. A part of me feared that if I went down that path, he would consume not only my mind, but the very essence of what I was.

"Then why bring me here?"

As I stated. You must see.

I felt the urge to walk forward, so I did. For the first few minutes, it was uneventful. Then, I came across a series of kiosks. Each one had a different remote controlled vehicle at it, and *only* that vehicle. I stepped up to the first, one for a car, and looked around it. There was a bloody piece of...something by the register. I didn't want to, but my hand moved forward and picked it up. A finger. When it moved I instinctively dropped it. It continued to wag at me on the floor.

I looked forward; all the other kiosks had similar bits and pieces of flesh at cash register. Each was moving or throbbing like the finger.

"No. You...didn't."

I ran to each, grabbing up the pieces, trying to put them together again. My hands and shirt were slick with blood, but I'd managed to piece together most of a head. I recognized it and immediately began to cry.

"K...kill...k-kill m-me." Victoria said, over and over again.

"You promised me!!"

All will serve. ALL.

I threw up. I kept throwing up until the vomit was dark and viscous. The black goo came pouring out of me, and showed no signs of stopping or slowing down. It consumed the ruined head of Victoria, and then began to eat away at me. Part of me felt glad that this would finally be over. That I would finally get release from this hell, release that I rightly deserved.

I was sorry, though. Sorry that I had failed Victoria. Sorry that I couldn't save her. Those were my last thoughts as the ooze overtook my face, and smothered me in blistering, acidic heat. Maybe this would truly be the end. Baal had broken me, completely and fully. Oblivion would come and I woul-

"Uncle David!"

Epilogue

Victoria felt like she was in a horrible, horrible nightmare. One moment she was being torn apart by that...*thing* while David looked on in horror, and the next she was floating. At least, it *felt* like floating. Almost as if she were suspended in a thick, tangible gas. She could still breathe, but she couldn't see anything.

Is this what being dead feels like? She didn't know. As far as she could tell, however, she still felt everything. She reached with her left hand and pinched her side. It hurt so much that she let out a small yelp. Which she heard.

The look in David's eyes, just before everything went black, haunted her. In all the time they'd spent together since this ordeal began, she had never seen him so hopeless.. He had given up, fully and completely. Was that what the thing had wanted? Why she had been let go?

Victoria slowly stirred and began to wake. She knew she was no longer in the endless void, because she could feel rocks pressing into her back and dirt sifting through her fingers as she began to sit up. At first she was afraid to open her eyes, but when nothing happened for a few seconds she finally dared to look.

Dawn. She could see the sun rising across the horizon, just cresting over forest that surrounded the back side of the mall. She glanced around, shielding herself from the sudden brightness.

Looking around, she realized she had woken up in a dirt lot that was the site of a future expansion of the mall.

There were several hills of dirt and piles of building material that was blocking her view, but if she remembered correctly, the mall would be on the other side.

Instead of getting up to check, she just sat there, running her fingers through the cold, soft earth. She was getting filthy, but it didn't matter. She took in a deep breath, filling her lungs with the fresh morning air, and let out a laugh despite herself. Weeping, she thanked whatever powers existed that she was free. Finally.

After sitting there for a few minutes, enjoying the sensations, she finally stood and moved towards the hill. The dirt was loose, which made climbing over it difficult, but once she was nearly over, she stopped and gasped.

Instead of the River Park Mall, there was a crater that went nearly as far as she could see. The entire building, and even some large chunks of the parking lot, was all gone. Several underground pipes were sheared off, dumping water into the crater. A few were spitting endless flames; obviously gas lines that had become ignited.

She was not surprised. Truth be told, she would have been more surprised if the mall were still standing. Randall's secret experiments had cost so many people their lives, but no one would believe her. If she told the truth, she would be branded insane and probably locked up.

She left her spot at the top of the hill, gently skidding downward until her feet were back on solid ground. She couldn't see her own face, but she knew she was a mess; her arms and legs were covered in dirt, and her clothing was ripped and torn.

She was the only survivor of...what? A gas leak? A random explosion? Whatever. It didn't matter. All that truly mattered was that it was over. She would feign ignorance to anyone who asked her for any details, and just say she had been knocked out and hadn't come to until well after everything was over. She had been running to catch the bus. Thrown out of harm's way like a rag doll. It was a believable story.

She just had to remain consistent. She practiced the story several times in her head; what she would say, and how she would say it, in case she was questioned several times. If she faltered, she could be in trouble. Hell, they might even try to find a way to pin this on her if they thought she was lying.

Panic seeped into her mind. Should she try and escape? Leave before anyone noticed her? Her time sheet was in the mall; there was no record of her having been there at all. She could say that she overslept for her shift. Blew it off. Tried to call and got no answer, so she'd decided to stay home.

"Hey! Hey you!"

Shit. Apparently *that* story wasn't going to work. She turned towards the voice, and saw a service truck of some kind parked near the edge of the crater, near one of the flaming gas lines. A man who looked like a utility worker was on a cell phone, and he had a look of permanent shock stuck on his face. He called to her again.

"Lady, are you okay?? Yeah," he spoke into the phone, "there's someone here. She looks hurt. You better send an ambulance too...I don't know! Send everyone!"

Her first story was going to have to do. She stumbled her way towards him, limping and trying to look more hurt than she actually was. He rushed to meet her halfway once he'd hung up the phone.

"Jesus, you look like you've been through hell and back, lady!"

He had no idea. "What...what happened?" She started to feel odd as he got closer. A sensation she couldn't quite describe.

"You don't know? Shit, looks like you were thrown clear of the blast. Looks like a gas explosion or...something." He seemed to doubt his own words as he looked back over the crater. "Only, no wreckage. Huh."

"I feel a bit dizzy."

He quickly turned back to her, rushing to her side. "You need to take it easy. I called 911, and they said that emergency services were on the way, including an ambulance. They told me to make sure you were alright."

"Please, come closer. I think I'm going to fall." She didn't say that. Why had she said that? The feeling was growing more intense, and her arm reached out for support. *I'm not doing this!!*

She tried to fight what her body was doing, but found it impossible. The man put his arm around her waist, offering support. Her right arm slid around his neck, while her left hand pulled the utility knife from his tool belt. It took him a moment to realize what she was doing.

"Hey, leave that alo-"

The ratchet of the blade as she extended it, and then subsequent stabbing of it into his neck, cut him off. She screamed, but her mouth didn't move. The man made a few garbled gurgling noises and fell to his knees, blood quickly pooling around him. Victoria's mouth curled into a smirk.

What the...what the fuck is going on?! She tried to wrestle control of her body back, but the sensation was now overwhelming. As if another mind was inside her body with her, pushing her back further and further; suppressing her thoughts and consciousness.

"All will serve."

No. This is impossible. You existed in the other world. You let me go!! David's promise to serve burned brightly in her memories, though not by her own doing. Over and over in her mind his concession, the one made to save her, played. Mocking her.

In particular, the promise he made Baal agree to, to restore her mind and body, and free her from harm, it kept showing her that moment exactly.

"You are restored. No harm has come to your mind or body. I will keep my word. However, there is too much to feel. To explore. I was going to use David, but he serves to entertain me. You, however, shall serve as a vessel."

I won't let you!!

"There is nothing to *let*. It is done." Bloody hands rifled over the corpse, pulling a set of keys from his pocket. Victoria's body moved to the truck, got in, and started the engine.

"So many have served as my conduit into existence. I can tell that the beings here, they shall serve well. My will be *done*."

Victoria tried to re-assert herself as her body shifted the truck into reverse, pulling back and then driving onto the nearby highway. Nothing happened. They continued to drive as the firetrucks and ambulances rolled past, lights and sirens blaring. When she realized there was nothing to do but play a witness to whatever was going to happen next, she did her best to withdraw into herself. Maybe she could find a way somehow to get free of this control.

"Oh no, you will witness." Her consciousness was pushed to the forefront. Still unable to act, but unable to turn away either.

Victoria's mouth curled into a grin, and then she broke out into a laugh as she turned the radio on. Beethoven's Overture from *Egmont* filled the cabin of the vehicle as they drove off towards the rising sun.

About The Author

    C.M.W. Hawkins is an American writer who lives in Alberta, Canada, with his wife and son. Imported back in 2004, he now considers the country to be his adopted homeland.

    When not writing about horrific trips to the mall...though one could argue that *all* trips to the mall are horrific...or fighting off nightmares from dark beings, he can be seen streaming video games live on his Twitch channel: http://www.twitch.tv/hawkzombie.

    An avid gamer, he prefers those with good story, good gameplay, or, preferably, both. He is particularly fond of games made with the RPG Maker engine, and lesser known indie titles.

    Of those lesser known titles, one of his favorites is the RPG *Geiken*.

www.ingramcontent.com/pod-product-compliance
Lightning Source LLC
Chambersburg PA
CBHW020616120726
47905CB00003B/811